"Honey, you've got to quit teasing my bull!"

"Teasing!" Bridget couldn't believe him.

"He's been bellowing for two hours. If you hadn't been teasing him, what are you doing sitting there in that tree just out of reach?"

She wailed, "Jeremy!"

He wasn't in the least bit of a hurry. He squinted his eyes at her. "Honey, did you leave anyone pining for you up there in Indian-er?"

"No!" She was becoming irritated.

"That's nice. What will you give me if I distract old Casanova?"

"My personal check for one million dollars."

J.R. scoffed. "Money! I don't need *money*!"

"What then?" A warm sensation curled around inside her. He would say he wanted her, and she'd simply have to agree—she had no choice.

"A kiss. A nice big one. All rescued maidens in distress kiss their rescuer. It's the rule."

Dear Reader,

Welcome to Silhouette. Experience the magic of the wonderful world where two people fall in love. Meet heroines who will make you cheer for their happiness, and heroes (be they the boy next door or a handsome, mysterious stranger) who will win your heart. Silhouette Romances reflect the magic of love—sweeping you away with books that will make you laugh and cry, heartwarming, poignant stories that will move you time and time again.

In the next few months, we're publishing romances by many of your all-time favorites, such as Diana Palmer, Brittany Young, Emilie Richards and Arlene James. Your response to these authors and other authors of Silhouette Romances has served as a touchstone for us, and we're pleased to bring you more books with Silhouette's distinctive medley of charm, wit and—above all—*romance*.

I hope you enjoy this book and the many stories to come. Experience the magic!

Sincerely,

Tara Hughes
Senior Editor
Silhouette Books

LASS SMALL
Snow Bird

Published by Silhouette Books New York

America's Publisher of Contemporary Romance

To my father, Richard Joseph Gittinger

SILHOUETTE BOOKS
300 E. 42nd St., New York, N.Y. 10017

ISBN: 0-373-08521-4

First Silhouette Books printing August 1987

America's Publisher of Contemporary Romance

Printed in the U.S.A.

Books by Lass Small

Silhouette Romance

An Irritating Man #444
Snow Bird #521

Silhouette Desire

Tangled Web #241
To Meet Again #322
Stolen Day #341
Possibles #356

LASS SMALL

started writing after attending a workshop where she received the following advice: "If you want to start writing, start." She did, and she's never looked back. In fact, she says, "I *love* writing. I love all aspects of it." When she's not writing the novels that have made her popular, she likes to spend her time reading, swimming and enjoying life with her husband and four children.

Chapter One

Down through the ages, the Taylors had always been noted for their dedicated enthusiasm. Actually, they were too loyal. For instance, in the last century, it was a good thing the Taylors were Yankees. If they'd been involved with the Southern Cause, they'd still be on some island in the Caribbean, clamoring for recognition in the United Nations, as the Government of the Confederate States in absentia.

Bridget was a Taylor through and through. In varying degrees, from approbation to despair, she'd heard it all her life: "You can tell that girl is a Taylor."

At twenty-two, she was pretty with swinging shining dark brown hair, blue eyes and an easy smile. Although not voluptuous, her body was nicely shaped.

Her voice was a rather attractive, foggy one with an occasional squeak. The year her high school teams seemed determined to win last place, Bridget was a cheerleader. She'd been sure that Taylor vocal power alone would lift the teams to victory. It had been a futile effort, and she'd almost ruined her vocal chords.

The summer after Bridget received her teaching degree from Ball State University, she was still living at home and job hunting. In the night, the family would waken as her father was racked by his tenacious cough.

Before her dad's annual physical, Bridget's mother called their doctor and asked him to pay close attention to her husband's cough. He'd had it much too long. The huffy doctor had replied stiffly, "Health is not a casual thing, Jean, and all aspects of it are under observation." Lawrence came home from his examination with a clean bill of health...and more cough medicine. A liquid Band-Aid.

Then a cousin wrote from Texas suggesting Lawrence come down there for the winter. They thought they could find the Taylors a reasonable place to rent, just west of San Antonio, and the bus service into the city was excellent.

Why not? Well, there were all kinds of problems, but for Taylors anything is solvable. So Jean signed a contract to teach school for the year, and it was decided the jobless Bridget would spend the winter in Texas with her father. However, they didn't leave until almost the middle of October when Indiana weather began to get mean. Bridget gradually realized that her father found it very difficult to leave her mother.

* * *

They finally arrived in San Antonio a little after four one sunny afternoon, to be welcomed by Lawrence's cousin. Sara Taylor Miner met them with her husband and two young sons. Like all Taylors, Sara and her sons were tall, slender and blue-eyed with brown hair; and her husband Ned could pass as kin.

Sara questioned with statements in a way peculiar to Texans. "We thought you'd just as soon go on out to your place today? We've gathered some cleaning things, some linens and a basic food supply."

They had a Texas-Mexican meal, before they drove to the rented house, "west of town." Lawrence inquired, "How far west?" Ned replied, "Just down the road a piece." It was forty miles.

Bridget found her two young cousins very similar to her brothers. She also discovered they still "fought" the Civil War in teasing. Only they called it The War Between the States. They'd duck down, hoping no one would see them riding in the same car with a . . . Yankee. They told her, since she was going to be there all winter, she should know that TEXAS is always said and written in capitals.

As the cousins teased, Bridget heard Sara say, "The house doesn't have a phone, but it *does* have an inside bath." The possibility hadn't occurred to Bridget, but the fact that having an inside bathroom was a plus did help to prepare them for the house.

It was almost dusk when they arrived. Fortunately, when the Miners had inspected the rental, they'd been shown exactly how to locate the house, otherwise they never would have found it.

The house was down a short lane and tucked among hackberry trees and scrub oak. It had a tin roof and unpainted siding with an open porch across the front. It was a typical Irish flat house, and the rent was cheap.

The floor was solidly built but only about six inches from the ground. One just stepped up onto the porch. They entered the living-dining room, which ran the width of the house. Beyond that room, the kitchen and bath were across from each other, separated by a short hallway leading to two small back bedrooms.

There was the fireplace on the living room side for cool evenings, or the occasional "blue norther," when the north winds turned everyone blue with the cold.

In looking around, they found there was no hot-water heater. Bath water would have to be heated in the kettle on the kitchen stove and carried into the bath.

The gas oven wasn't vented, and it had no thermostat. That would make baking an adventure. The refrigerator was fifty years old. It stood up on legs, and there was a two-ice-tray freezer compartment. It would have to be defrosted. And there was a kerosene lamp.

To one side of the yard was an old shed enclosed with a wooden slat fence in reasonable repair. Near the house was a water tower, which squatted next to the windmill. Two tubs and a scrub board stood on a bench under the water tower. Sara winced. "Your laundry room." Ned helped them figure out how to start and stop the water flow. It was interesting.

The Miners said the last tenants had left owing rent and leaving the place a mess. Being Taylors by either genes or osmosis, the Miner cousins had come prepared to work. With six of them, the sparsely furnished little house was soon cleaned.

The curtains were taken down and put to soak in a tub out under the water tower. The dirty mattresses were carried out to the shed. The walls were wiped down and the floors mopped, as Sara put around lids of cockroach powder. Then the tacky wicker table and chairs on the porch were scrubbed. The three-cushioned, lumpy, old brown sofa was next. And the two boys gathered armloads of fallen limbs, which they broke into lengths to fit the fireplace.

With their cleaning done, the cousins built an initiating fire. They settled down on the clean, bare floor to open the champagne and gobble down the sandwiches Sara had brought.

While they were eating the Taylors heard this first: "If you use the kitchen oven, open a window, the stove isn't vented, and you could be asphyxiated. When you walk along the track—the gravel road—watch for snakes. And never picnic or drive along a dry river bed. Rains from far away can send a flood runoff down such a bed, and you could be caught unaware and drowned." The Miners gave the two new natives a marked map of the area. When they left at midnight, Bridget felt she'd known the cousins all her life.

Their second afternoon in residence, Bridget had just taken very carefully watched cookies from the clean tricky oven, when a pickup slammed into their side yard. She was delighted to have a neighborly visit so soon and hurried to the door with a big smile.

The visitor had just reached his fist to hammer on the door when Bridget opened it, startling them both. They stared at each other for a telling minute of intense awareness. He frowned as he cuffed back his Stetson from his forehead.

He was taller than she and somewhat older, about twenty-four or -five. His shoulders were wide, and he had a lean hard body. Under his cowboy hat, Bridget could see he was a blond. His brows and lashes were sunbleached and most attractive. There were laugh or sun-squint wrinkles at the corners of his clear eyes. They were a strange blue-green and...furious! How could such a blond look like a black thundercloud?

Bridget's soft lips parted in surprise, and the stranger's gaze fell to them as his hands reached out, in conditioned reflex, to grab her shoulders. He almost shook her as he snarled, "You get those dogs penned up! Do you hear me?"

She was astonished. Why would he be so angry with her? After a try or two, standing there in his hard grip, she squeaked, "W-what dogs?"

"Those!" he grated and turned her effortlessly to follow his pointing finger. She looked where he pointed and saw two, *huge*, emaciated hounds that were watching ominously from the trees. He continued, "and if they savage my sheep one more time, I'll shoot them! Do you understand me?"

After pointing at the dogs, his hand had returned to her shoulder so that she stood between his hands. He frowned even *more*, if that could be possible.

Then his hands became oddly gentle and his thumbs almost absently moved in a caressing way as he shook his head and said, "You don't look the type at all." Leaving her completely baffled, he stormed off the porch to his pickup, ripped open the door, flung himself into it, and spun out of the yard.

Bridget couldn't believe it. She'd just met the dream of any woman in a strange land, and he was angry! He was furious about those dogs. No one had said they came with the place. She was afraid of dogs. She was supposed to capture...those monsters? How in the world was she going to pen them?

Well, if that angry man thought she could do it, then she supposed she could. She took a deep breath, stood bravely straight, and stepped off the porch.

They didn't attack.

First she tried whistling the classic two-note call while she snapped her fingers and said in a passably firm manner, "Here, boy." No good. The beasts just watched her in a dull-eyed way. Their bones showed through their short-haired, purple-cast coats. She went inside and took supper's hamburger from the refrigerator and returned. She opened the gate to the shed enclosure, then approached the dogs as she broke off some of the meat to lure them into the shed.

It didn't work out the way she'd planned. The dogs were starving. With the first indication of food, they simply ran over her, snatched the meat and wolfed it down. Then they stood trembling nervously and salivating as they waited anxiously for more food.

Bridget was terrified! She watched the hunger-induced saliva around their mouths and decided the dogs were rabid. With her heart pounding in her ears, she knew she couldn't call her father. With two such great animals, he too would be torn down. Her mother needed him. So did her young brothers.

But she was a Taylor! While she bravely refused to endanger her father, she considered how she could survive. She would have to go past the dogs to get to the house. Even if she was bitten, the serum would save her, if her jugular vein was protected. How could she do that?

Her shirt was too flimsy to be of any use. She slid off her jeans and wrapped that heartier material tightly around her throat and lower face so only her horrified blue eyes peeked out. She began to creep toward the porch. The dogs whined and made throat noises as they followed along, trying to tell her how hungry they were, and that the hamburger hadn't been enough.

It took an age for her to edge that two hundred miles, or fifty feet, to the house. She finally leaped onto the porch, snatched the door open, dashed inside, slammed it shut and leaned against it with a soul-wrenched sob. She was safe.

"What in *hell* is going on?"

In her blue-jean-wrapped throat, T-shirt and wild flowered underwear, Bridget looked over her shoulder to her baffled father. "The dogs..." she gasped, almost fainting in relief. "The dogs have rabies."

Lawrence frowned down at her and went to lean on one of the windowsills that overlooked the porch. His voice softened as he began to realize how thoroughly frightened she'd been. "No, honey, they're not rabid...just hungry."

As her trembling hands unwrapped her jeans, and her wet-noodle legs attempted to slide back into them, she told him, "I'm supposed to pen them. They've been after sheep and..."

"No wonder. What do we have to feed them?"

Still rather dazed, she asked, "Chicken livers?"

"That'll do for starters."

Lawrence went out and talked to the dogs with sympathy. They tried their best to reply. He firmly disciplined them as Bridget handed the livers out through an only partially opened door. He fed the dogs carefully in turn, as he led them to the shed. When that gate was safely closed, Bridget brought pans of milk with beaten eggs. Lawrence slowly fed the starving dogs; then he took them bowls of water.

That night, tucked into her bedroll on the naked squeaky springs of her bed, Bridget spent quite a good many dreams with the thunderheaded man. She explained to him about the dogs, and she tried to get him to quit being angry and act as dream men are supposed to act.

The next morning, she put bread chunks in pans and added milk and bacon drippings. She slid the pans through the slats of the shed. The dogs greeted her with wagging tails and soft "talking" whines, but she wasn't won over.

After that, dressed in old jeans and a Ball State T-shirt, she consulted the map and set out for the store. She walked a little over a mile along the gravel road, which wandered through the stunted trees. In the beginning of the TEXAS "winter," there were dried weeds along the sides and down the middle of the double track. The silence was broken only by the soft breeze and the twitterings of birds. Now that she knew the dogs couldn't get out, the walk was very pleasant.

The general store and gas station had been built some long time ago at a crossroad. In fact, the road had been built to bend past a great old live oak which had shaded the road, the side yard and the entrance to the store. But three or four years before, lightning had struck down the tree's heart, twisting it apart in an awesome way. It was a nine-day wonder before the road crew showed up to clear it away. Any number of viewers of the dead oak had said the same thing: "That's what 'thunderstruck' looks like."

Mrs. Smith, who ran the store, made them leave the shattered trunk. "It'll remind folks about the wrath of God!" she said, but she never explained why God should have been so angry with that old oak.

The birds had gradually moved in, the woodpeckers went to work keeping it tidy, and it was a lovely sculpture, pleasing to the eye. But the parking area was made of white rock mixed with crushed shell from the Gulf of Mexico. Without the tree, the sun beat down, reflecting light into the store in an unbearable way.

As Bridget went inside, the reflection captured her attention. She smiled cheerfully to say, "Good morning" to a glum Mrs. Smith who sat behind the counter by the door.

She returned Bridget's greeting with a grunt. She eyed her customer with her wrinkles set in a sour face. Her thin white hair was screwed up in a tight bun, and in her ears hung graceful, golden, Gordian knot earrings.

Cheerleaders are outgoing people not easily put off, and so are *ex*-cheerleaders. Bridget put up her hand to shield her eyes from the sun's relentless light. "Doesn't that glare give you a headache?"

"Sometimes," granted Mrs. Smith, eyeing the "B.S." on Bridget's T-shirt.

With two such contacts with the natives, Bridget wondered about the fabled TEXAS friendliness. Undeterred, she prodded further, "That tree was huge! You must miss it very much."

"I do," was the grudging agreement.

"You might consider putting up poles and laying snow fencing horizontally about twenty feet up. It would cut the glare until you could grow more trees."

"Snow fencing?" Mrs. Smith was dubious.

Bridget smiled. "The Montgomery Ward catalogue has it. They'd ship it here to TEXAS, although it might astonish them to do so."

Mrs. Smith gave a flicker of a smile with a slight but fascinating rearrangement of wrinkles, but she remained silent.

Bridget gave up. "Perhaps you could help me?"

Mrs. Smith watched her, still silently, not offering any encouragement.

"Who is the blond man about twenty-five . . . nice looking, if he weren't such a *thundercloud*!"

Interest sparking, Mrs. Smith replied instantly, "That would be Jeremy Robert Winsome. Most folks call him J.R. Why do you want him?"

"He came by yesterday just furious about two dogs, and . . ."

"With good cause!" Her voice was stern.

Bridget said in her defense, "Well, we didn't know they came with the house, and we hadn't seen them when we moved in two days a—"

Mrs. Smith frowned and interrupted, "You just moved in? Haven't you all been there all summer?"

"Oh no. This is only our third day there. But that Mr. Winsome—"

"What happened to the couple that was there?"

Bridget replied patiently, "I don't know." Then she tried again, "But Mr. Winsome—"

"Then those aren't your dogs?" Mrs. Smith straightened up and became alert.

"Good heavens, no! I have a horror of dogs!"

There was a sound in the back of the store but the strong light, cast up by the white parking lot, was so blinding that the back of the store was very dark. Bridget tried to shade her eyes as she squinted to look into the shadows. "Is someone here?"

"It's probably Jim in the back room. Who is the 'we' that moved in? You and . . . ?"

"My father, Lawrence Taylor. I'm Bridget."

Her curiosity was now lively. "Where you folks from?"

"Indiana. We're staying for the winter."

"Just you and your daddy?"

"Yes." Bridget smiled a little, amused by the friendly change in the bald interrogation from Mrs. Smith. "Mother and my two younger brothers stayed in Indiana. Mother is teaching there and my brothers are in high school. They'll be down at Christmastime." She decided she might as well tell it all. "My dad has had a very stubborn cough. So mother convinced him to take his sabbatical now, and we came down—"

The old lady raised her eyebrows. "Sabbatical?"

"He teaches at the university."

"Oh?"

"So," she continued her recital, "we hope to get him really healthy here in your good sunshine this winter, and he'll work on his book."

"He's writing a book?"

"On the Etruscans."

"Etruscans, huh." She paused and regarded Bridget a silent minute. "It sounds like you've got a nice family."

"They all are."

"Then why would a nice little girl like you run around with B.S. on her shirt that way?"

"That's for Ball State!" Bridget touched her nicely rounded chest and looked offended.

"What's Ball State?"

Bridget exclaimed, "That's a University at Muncie, Indiana! It's a very fine university. You've seen Ball jars? The university is named for the Ball family. It has the only architectural college in Indiana, a very fine nursing school, and among other colleges, it has one of the best of all teachers' colleges.''

"You old enough to be in college?'' Mrs. Smith sounded doubtful.

"I've graduated! I'm a teacher, certified and licensed to teach elementary education.'' She bowed.

"Well, I declare to goodness! Element'ry teacher huh?''

"Yes.'' They smiled at each other. Then Bridget took a deep breath and said, "About my problem, Mr. Winsome.''

"The thundercloud?''

"What a *hateful* man he must be!''

"Terrible, but ninety-eight percent of the women find him irresistible.'' The skin around Mrs. Smith's eyes wrinkled, and there was another scraping sound from the back of the store.

Bridget was so involved in telling Mrs. Smith her problem that she didn't even try to see the source of the sound . . . which was Jeremy Robert Winsome.

He felt uncomfortable, having realized he'd vented his fury over the dogs on an innocent girl, whose silhouette against the glare was proof she was nicely shaped indeed. He listened with growing discomfort as she continued in her attractive, foggy voice.

"He told me to *pen up those dogs!* And I had no idea what he was talking about! So he pushed me around. . . .''

"He didn't!'' Mrs. Smith was enjoying the plight of their eavesdropper.

"Oh, he didn't actually hurt me, but he was very rude.''

"Sounds like J.R. all right."

A can fell from a shelf in back. Bridget didn't pay any attention, but Mrs. Smith rubbed a hand over her mouth to erase a smile.

Bridget warmed to her story. "And you've never seen two bigger or meaner looking dogs!"

Mrs. Smith made a sympathetic sound.

"Wait until you hear what I did!" Bridget could laugh...now. And she told her dramatic story about being sure the dogs had rabies...reaching the safety of the house, a complete shambles! "With my jeans wrapped around my throat and standing there in my B.V.D.s!" Bridget laughed so Mrs. Smith had to laugh too, but hers was gentle.

Jeremy wished he could have been there.

"Then after all that emotional drama, Dad went out and they were like lambs! Starving lambs. But what do we do with them? Apparently we can't turn them loose, and it would be cruel to keep them penned. Mr. Winsome just said to pen them."

"We'll just put a call in to Little John." Mrs. Smith pushed up her lower lip and nodded as she agreed with herself.

"Little John as in *Robin Hood*?"

"His name is really Jack Small, but everyone calls him Little John. I'll send him over to fetch them dogs as soon as he can."

"What will happen to them? Dad says they're nice dogs."

"I don't know. You can ask Little John when you see him. You'll like *him*." Mrs. Smith took gleeful pleasure in slightly emphasizing that. "Little John is a gentleman."

"Not like some."

"Right." Mrs. Smith agreed, knowing J.R. flinched. "Couple of things you should know, honey, being a Yankee. If you turn on gas, be sure there's a window open, watch out for snakes and stay out of dry river beds. Anything else I can help you with?"

Bridget nodded and said, "We could use two three-quarter mattresses. Those in the house were so dirty we put them in the shed."

"I got a couple in the loft you can borrow."

"Terrific! And dog food, of course, and a bicycle?"

"No car?"

"No, the budget won't stretch that far."

"How about a little Honda scooter?"

"I'm not sure." Bridget frowned.

"We'll check it out, okay? Anything else?"

"Mousetraps."

"Got mice, huh."

Bridget laughed. Why else would she want mousetraps?

"I'll send Miss Pru with Little John when he brings you the mattresses. It *should* be Mrs. Pru," she confided, "all the kittens she's had! You can use her for the winter. Okay? She's a visitor. Now let's see about the Honda."

Jeremy couldn't believe he'd heard right. Mrs. Smith was going to let the Honda go? He watched the two women go over to the garage where Mrs. Smith wheeled out her beloved antique. It wasn't one to straddle, but rather like a scooter with a seat at the back and a place in front of the seat for feet.

J.R. lurked in the store's shadows, straining to watch and wishing he could hear. Between the two women, there were explanations and discussions. Bridget was obviously doubtful.

Explaining all the while, Mrs. Smith started the putt-putt and eased it into action. Bridget timidly did the same, cautiously riding in a gentle turn. Then she drove more boldly and, finally, with some flair. J.R. watched and smiled to see Bridget smile. He saw the two women shake hands on some kind of bargain, then they returned, as he retreated out of sight.

Mrs. Smith knew he was still there. "Wait here, honey," she told Bridget, "I'll collect your things." Still talking, she gathered bread, milk, dog food, more hamburger and cheese—and she walked right by J.R. as if he was invisible. "Those other people who lived out there never did come in here. Very unfriendly. I'm glad they've gone; but I can't tell you, honey, how sorry I am you were forced to cope with them dogs."

"That's very nice of you, Mrs. Smith." Bridget paid for the groceries and helped sack the food. "I did survive. Thank you for everything. And I'll take very good care of your Honda."

Mrs. Smith walked outside with her. "I know you will."

J.R. watched them strap the groceries on the back of the scooter. Bridget waved and rode carefully away.

He was waiting when Mrs. Smith came inside. She went behind the counter and sat again on her high stool. He leaned his hip against the counter, tipped back his Stetson and scolded her. "You *could* have said you didn't know who 'Old Thundercloud' might be!" He mimicked, "Sounds like J.R. all right!"

Unruffled, she greeted him, "Hello, J.R. I thought you might still be here."

"You knew good and well I was! You walked right by me!"

"I did?" Her face was so innocent.

"You sold her your Honda?"

"Loaned it to her."

He gasped. "Loaned it?"

Defensively she explained, "I did it for the school board."

"Hah! What's the school board got to do with you being a soft touch?"

She denied that. "I am not! But we need a substitute teacher in the element'ry grades."

His sea-blue-green eyes laughed. "Why'd you tell her all those terrible things about me!"

"All true."

"I really botched it, didn't I. I feel like a snake."

"She's probably more afraid of snakes than she is of starving...rabid...dogs." She ground that into him.

"That poor little girl. I wish I could have been there."

"To help."

He slanted a wicked grin. "To see her in her drawers with her jeans around her head."

"Men."

"Honey, you love us all."

"Not all the time."

Chapter Two

The next morning, as J.R. drove past the crossroads store, he saw Little John wrestling a mattress onto the top of his station wagon under the critical eye of Mrs. Smith. J.R. tooted his horn and drove on by, "failing" to hear Little John's shout for help.

It was almost nine o'clock when Little John drove into the Taylor yard. He'd been feeling somewhat irritated until he saw Bridget open the door, then his whole day brightened. He took off his Stetson, smiled and said, "Hi, I'm Little John. Smitty sent me. She said you'd give me a cup of coffee while Miss Pru gets settled?" He reached into the back seat of his rusty, disreputable looking station wagon and lifted out a plump, limp calico cat who hung on his hand and gazed around with lazy interest.

Bridget held open the door, smiled wider and said softly, "Come in. Dad's still sleeping."

As she led the way into the kitchen, Little John glanced around the clean, tidy, but rather bare living room and hung his hat on the wooden rack by the door. He followed Bridget into the kitchen as he made Miss Pru comfortable in his arms. The cat absent-mindedly purred a bit to please him as she continued to look around.

"You put some butter on her paw and by the time she licks it off, she feels at home. Everybody does that. Smitty claims that's the reason Miss Pru doesn't mind moving around from place to place. She knows she'll get a pawful of butter."

Bridget grinned as she scooped some butter onto a scrap of paper towel and smeared it on the paw Little John held ready. Miss Pru watched, alert and eager. He put the cat down on the floor and smoothed her fur. She moved briefly under his hand to acknowledge his courtesy before she daintily began to lick the butter from her paw.

Little John's smile was white in his plain, tan, friendly face. "Speaking of paws...I understand your daddy's not been too well?"

She grinned at his word play. "He's just run down. His doctor says he's sound. We figure he just needs to rest and build his body up again. That's why we're here. Your climate had better live up to its reputation and work its miracle on him."

"No problem." He sipped the hot coffee, which he really didn't want.

"Do you work around here?" She wondered at what, with that awful looking car.

His eyes on his cup, he replied, "I'm Smitty's errand boy."

"Oh." She thought he was rather old to still be an errand boy. He had to be at least twenty-five or twenty-six.

"And marshal for this area." He looked up, his eyes dancing with humor. "Although Smitty doesn't recognize that I have that job, too. You see, Smitty's cousin to my grandmother. She never did have any kids of her own and when I was born, she told my mama, 'This one's mine.' Mama was touched to her heart, thinking Smitty needed a special child to love and, of course, I was precious."

"Of course."

"But what Smitty really wanted was a free errand boy. I'll tell her, 'I can't stop by! There's been a bank held up!' 'Where?' she'll ask. 'Bandara!' 'Good,' she'll say. 'Take these things by Agnes's on your way.'"

"So she made you come here today."

"Had Smitty bothered to mention who it was for, I'd have been a lot more willing." He put down his cup. "I've got some cream for Miss Pru's first saucer. After that you can give her just plain old milk."

"Miss Pru, you're being hoodwinked!"

The cat gave Bridget a tolerant look.

Little John brought the cream from the car, and they watched for a minute as Miss Pru daintily lapped it from a saucer by the stove. Little John said, "I'll get the mattresses." As he stepped from the porch, he saw

the sun glint briefly from field glasses up on the hill,
and he recognized the outline of a horse, almost ob-
scured by a mesquite tree. Little John thought that was
interesting. Gus was J.R.'s horse, so J.R. was watching from the hill.

Smitty had told Little John all about J.R.'s en-
counter with Bridget, of his slinking around in the
shadows during the tale of woe, and he'd heard her
opinion of Old Thundercloud.

From the top of the hill, J.R. saw Little John come
off the porch and unlash the first mattress, lifting it
with a show-offy effortlessness. Little John was J.R.'s
best friend, but not right then. J.R. just wished Bridget could have seen how Little John had struggled with
that same damned mattress at the store. Nothing like
a pretty girl to make Little John's muscles work at
peak level. J.R. sat there, his elbows braced on his
knees, his eyes glued to the glasses as he ground his
teeth and was grim.

The curtains were still down from the windows in
Bridget's bare little room. Newspapers were taped to
the panes. Little John smiled to himself. A city girl, he
thought, nobody anywhere around out here, but she
wasn't taking any chances. She was modest.

She took her sleeping bag off the springs, and he
eased the mattress into place on the old iron bed-
stead. In the next room they heard Lawrence racked
by coughing. Little John watched Bridget's face flinch
at the sound. "I've heard worse," he told her softly.

She thought how nice he was.

They leaned the other mattress in the hall against
the wall. Then Little John went out and backed the

station wagon close to the gate of the small shed yard where the dogs were penned. There was a wire cage in the back of his wagon. Bridget stood next to the gate. "What will happen to them?" she asked as he got out of the car.

"We'll advertise first. We suspect they're valuable animals and might have been stolen. No owner would abandon such a breed of dogs."

"If they're not claimed?"

"Then we'll try to find them a place, away from sheep of course." He opened the back of the wagon.

"They won't be... killed?" She wasn't fond of them, but she hated to see anything wasted, especially useful lives.

"I think someone will claim them." He ordered the dogs up on the tailgate. They jumped with willing familiarity into the caged back. "See? They're used to travelling this way." Little John closed the end up and latched it.

Then, knowing J.R. watched, Little John deliberately stood around in friendly conversation with Bridget. Not flirting, just being friendly. No other girl had ever claimed J.R.'s riveted attention. A dose of jealousy would do J.R. some good, it'd be a new experience for him. Little John smiled. It might not hurt for this to get back to Bernice either. "You'll have to meet Bernice Peters. She's about your age and she knows everyone around, so you'll get acquainted easier."

"Is she one of the ninety-eight percent Mrs. Smith says find J.R. irresistible?"

He paused thoughtfully and replied with typical honesty, "For now." Then he went on to caution, "Watch out for snakes. Don't step off a rock ledge or over a log without looking. And have a window open since your stove isn't vented, and stay out of dry river beds. They look like nice places to picnic, but the reason they're cleared like that is because they are periodically flooded. Too often the runoff is from far away. The sun will be out, no sign of a storm, maybe only a little thunder away off in the distance, and all of the sudden here comes a ten-foot wall of water! We lose a lot of Yankees that way."

After Little John took the dogs away, Bridget went inside. Her dad was up, yawning and pottering around the kitchen in his robe. Bridget took over making his breakfast, and he inquired, "So the dogs are gone?"

She nodded. "Little John's a Marshal. He thinks the dogs were stolen and abandoned."

"That would be very possible. I like the cat."

"That's Miss Pru. Why don't you take breakfast out on the porch in the sun? It's warm there."

"That would be nice." As Lawrence ate, he and Bridget discussed what color to paint the wicker and decided a greyed-brick-red would be attractive.

They found out Miss Pru could push the screen door open as she too came outside. They were watchful to see if she would wander off, but it wasn't long before she hooked her claws into the screen, pulled open the door and darted back inside before it slammed. Very practiced. A clever cat.

Bridget helped her dad put his mattress on his bed, and they made up both beds, using from Cousin Sara's

supplies. Then, dressed, Lawrence went out into the
gentle sunshine and tinkered with the Honda. It was
like one he'd once had long ago.

The curtains had been soaking in cold-water soap
suds for several days. Not having a water heater,
Bridget started heating buckets of water for the wash-
ing. Cousin Sara, being a Taylor, had brought a
clothesline and of course she'd remembered a pack-
age of clothes pins. Lawrence strung the line between
some of the scrub oak trees, with Miss Pru batting at
the rope ends.

After lunch, when Lawrence had ridden the Honda
to the store with some letters to mail, J.R. drove into
the yard with his pickup full of wood. Bridget looked
at that gorgeous man and had to breathe through her
mouth and swallow several times as all sorts of exci-
tations wove through her insides. She didn't smile
back but just looked at him. She disciplined herself to
look haughty and queenly, but instead she really
looked very pretty and big-eyed.

J.R. climbed out of his truck, took off his Stetson
and smiled in his most beguiling way. Then Bridget's
eyes became enormous as a big lean nondescript
brown dog slinked from the truck and sat down beside J.R., its calm eyes on Bridget.

"Don't fret," J.R. hastened to tell her. "He
wouldn't hurt a flea, unfortunately." He added that,
and the laugh lines deepened around his eyes. "Look,
honey..."

Against the thrill of hearing him call her that, she
said, "Don't call me honey."

"Sweety?" He waited for permission which didn't come and he added, very amused, willing to accept help, "Darling? Little bit . . . ?"

"With a vocabulary like that—" her tone was censoring "—no wonder you're irresistible to ninety-eight percent of the women."

"I strongly suspect that you number yourself in the resistible two percent?" His eyes danced in humor. He lounged by his truck, so amused by her, and so full of himself that she had to smile. He coaxed, "I made a terrible mistake accusing you of neglecting those poor dogs. You do remember that I did say you didn't look the type? I'm sorry, Miss Taylor, honey."

"I accept your apology, Mr. Winsome," she replied with gracious coolness.

He grinned at her for a minute then remembered why he was there. "Little John noticed you didn't have wood for your fireplace, and Mrs. Smith heard this wood was going begging? It would be a favor if you'd take it?" J.R. stood straight and put his Stetson back on. He looked marvelous.

Feeling a bit boggled, Bridget's tongue didn't work exactly as it should. "Why . . . that's very nice of her . . . and you." She did have to add that.

He looked around. "Where would you like the wood put?"

Dragging her eyes away from him, she too looked around. "I . . . I don't know."

"Well." He gestured, indicating his plan. "How about some inside, some there on the porch and the rest handy by that tree?"

"That...would be fine. But if you just dump it, we could stack it later."

"All I've done all day is just sit around." On that hill, watching her. "And I'll never sleep tonight if I don't get *some* kind of exercise. So you'd be doing me a kindness if you'd allow me to stack this little bit of wood. And if you have any other chores? That would be a help to me."

Bridget smiled, then laughed. What a confidence man he was! She tried to help stack, but he was appalled. He claimed it hurt his very heart to see a lady stack wood. She could scrub floors, that didn't count, but stacking wood was a man's job. She was supposed to sit there so he could see how pretty she looked, a Yankee in the TEXAS sun. Did she know that TEXAS was always capitalized? She was supposed to admire his strength and muscles, exclaiming softly... but with *some* control. She was to try not to let her admiration get out of hand, although he realized that was a lot to ask. He was so sassy that Bridget again laughed out loud.

When he told her the dog's name was Cassius because he had a lean and hungry look, she gave the man a closer study. "You read Shakespeare?"

"All Westerners know the Bible and Shakespeare. Weight was a problem in olden times, when space in wagons was at a premium. Reading material mostly came down to the *Bible* and *Complete Works of Shakespeare*. And when you think about it: what more masterful stories?"

Bridget agreed, her eyes watching his movements, her body reacting to his astonishingly. She could not stand around and watch him. J.R. was teasing when he'd said she'd have to control herself, but it was true. Reluctantly, she returned to the scrub board by the water tank. She kept her eyes from him so she wasn't aware how often his eyes turned her way.

When he'd finished with the wood, she offered him a glass of lemonade, which he quickly accepted. She sat with him on the porch while he slowly sipped it, making it last. Their silence was easy for him, but a little awkward for her. "Tell me about..." What? "Little John."

He studied her with a frown. He wasn't about to talk about Little John! Instead he told her about the dog, Cassius. "He's a great snake dog."

"Snakes! Everyone warns us about snakes!" She frowned as she glanced around.

"We do have a few. And I noticed you walked to the store and—"

"How did you know that?"

He ignored her question. "We're never that close to the ground. We're either up on a horse, or on a truck or in a car. Don't walk around carelessly, keep an eye out on the road, open a window if the gas is on and stay out of—"

"Dry river beds," she finished for him.

Bridget did watch for snakes, for a while. But she didn't see any sign of a snake...that she recognized. Gradually she lost her fear and even grew rather careless. She decided all the snake talk was their way of being funny at a stranger's expense. A kind of "new boy" joke. To be the brunt of jokes rather irritated her.

A Mr. Samuel Hughes came by the Taylors' on Friday. He sat on one of the recently painted, fortunately dry, greyed-brick-red wicker porch chairs, visiting with Lawrence and Bridget in the soft evening. It turned out he was a member of the school board, and they needed a substitute the next week? "Our fourth-grade teacher, Miz Moore has to go see her daddy who isn't feel hisself a-tall."

Bridget had her transcript of grades from Ball State with her along with her other papers, which she gave to Mr. Hughes. It wasn't until he was ready to leave that Bridget realized his gentle visit had been her interview.

The gentleman drew a careful map so that she could find the school, and he inquired if it would be convenient for her to be there about eight-thirty or so on Monday morning?

He was so grateful and, as salary was never mentioned, Bridget wondered if her substituting would be considered as a neighborly favor. She thought perhaps the school district was poor and people just "helped out" as needed. Well, if that was so, she'd do it. It was good experience and surely they'd give her a recommendation.

That weekend she painted the front door a bright mustard, and she rode the route to the school twice to be sure she wouldn't get lost when Monday came. Then, on Monday morning, wearing a crisp blue shirtwaist and a sweater on the cool October morning, she mounted the scrubbed Honda and rode se-

dately toward the school, pretending she wasn't
nervous. She rode down the two-rut track that wandered through the dry weeds. Almost at the school she
came upon the snake. It was enormous! And it lay
carelessly coiled there in the left-hand rut.

Bridget braked to a halt, her feet automatically
bracing the Honda as she stared in horror with her
heart beating in her ears. Although she was immobile
for an endless time, Bridget knew she had to go on to
the school and help out. Taylor genes demanded that.
She stared fascinated with the horror of an actual
snake. As the time slowly passed, Bridget gradually
realized the snake was dead.

One silly corner of her mind was running at sev-
enty-eight RPM. So there really were snakes! The natives hadn't been teasing.

Her heart finally settled back down into her chest,
beating slow dull thumps, but her legs gave way. She
abruptly sat on the Honda seat. Then a whispering
sound from behind made her jerk around in renewed
fright, eyes wide and mouth open.

A very neat green Porsche had already stopped in
back of her, and emerging from it was J.R. Winsome.
He was wearing a suntan-colored suit, a cream shirt
and a black string tie. He grinned and said, "Good
morning, honey."

She managed to croak, "Don't call me honey."

"I stopped by your place to carry you to school, but
your daddy said you'd already left. My, but you're
eager. You'll get there before Mr. Borg."

"Who is Mr. Borg?"

"The custodian."

"Oh."

There was a silence; then he inquired, really very gently, "Run out of gas?"

"Uh...no." It would be terrible for a Taylor to admit she'd been scared out of her shoes.

"Admiring the view?" He looked around and pretended his eyes had just found the snake. "By jingo, an earthworm! You don't see many unless it rains." His eye-crinkles deepened.

"That's a *snake*!"

"No!" He pretended shock as he walked over, hunkered down, sitting easily on his heels, as he studied the snake. "It's just a little bitty one. Want the rattles?"

She gasped, "No!" and immediately realized her brothers would be jubilant to get them, but she refused to consider that. He found a stick, put it in a coil of the five footer and tossed it from the road. She shuddered.

"I'm glad you're keeping those pretty little eyes peeled, honey, but when they're dead like that, you can go on by them. Let's put your Honda over there by the fence, out of the way. No one will bother it there and risk Mrs. Smith getting cross at them. We'll pick it up after school."

Stiff with independence, and the residue of fright, she replied, "No, thank you. I would rather go by myself."

He read her exactly. "Okay. Then I'll follow you."

"I go very slowly and I doubt that car can even idle that slowly."

Showing how far he would go to accommodate a
lady, he smiled. "Then I'll meet you there." He
climbed into the Porsche, drove that elegant car carelessly around through the rough dry weeds, then
slowly drove along the track until he was out of sight.
He was careful not to raise any dust for her to have to
ride through.

J.R. was waiting for her in the schoolyard, leaning
against his car, his arms folded. He spoke to almost
everyone and even the littlest kids smiled and called to
him.

There were a lot of curious glances Bridget's way,
but no one stared. J.R. moved from the Porsche to
help Bridget with her Honda and offer to carry her
folder and lunch sack. That made some of the boys
raise their eyebrows, and there were smothered giggles from a few of the girls.

Bridget wished J.R. would just go about his business and leave her alone. She was nervous enough
without him hanging around. But he took her arm and
walked with her through the curious students and into
the school. Taking off his hat, he continued right to
the principal's office! She hinted firmly, "Thank you,
Mr. Winsome. Goodbye." He opened the door for
her.

The principal, a mild, slightly overweight man, rose.
"Well, hello there, J.R. Where'd you find that pretty
little girl?"

Bridget winced at not being treated in a businesslike manner, but J.R. grinned and introduced the
principal, "Honey, this is George Cleaver. George,

this is Bridget Taylor? She's the little Yankee Sam called you about substituting for Many Ann?"

"Don't tell me this little girl is out of college!" George chuckled indulgently.

Being called honey, Yankee, and having her age, and therefore her qualifications, questioned edged Bridget's temper, especially since she was probably substituting as a favor. But, she reminded herself, they were undoubtedly trying to be kind. Rather formally she replied, "Yes, sir. I was graduated last spring from Ball State University in Indiana and I have all my papers..."

Mr. Cleaver waved them aside. "Oh, Sam already interviewed you. J.R. vouches for you, and Mrs. Smith says you'll do just fine." When Bridget looked puzzled, Mr. Cleaver explained, "J.R. and Mrs. Smith are on the school board?"

J.R. still didn't leave but walked beside her to the classroom. He went ahead of her, and blocked the door as he said in a carrying voice, "Here's your room. You've got the nicest kids in the whole building!" He waited as they heard a hushed, excited scramble of kids, then ushered Bridget into the room. All sixteen children were sitting at their desks, with their hands folded and laughter dancing in their eyes.

"See?" J.R. asked Bridget. "Didn't I tell you? Angels, every one." The class giggled. Then he spoke to them. "Now you all know that Mrs. Moore's daddy's not been well? So she's gone to visit him for a time. And your school board, having your best interests at heart, *imported* Miss Taylor clear down from Indiana to teach you this week. She talks kinda funny,

but I do know you'll make her feel at home and behave yourselves. You hear me?'' There was a murmur
of agreement and the kids looked at Bridget with lively
interest. J.R. said he might get back later, and he left.

The absent Mrs. Moore was obviously a paragon.
She had study sheets laid out, lessons prepared, and
instructions that were so clear and easy to follow that
Bridget wondered who they generally had to depend
on to substitute.

The children were not as bad as some fourth grad-
ers, and a whole lot better than most, but Bridget was
very glad to see that day end. She rode the Honda
home to find her dad waiting on the porch with iced
tea for her. She sat down gratefully, kicked off her
shoes and stretched as she told him about the day.

Lawrence's day, too, had been interesting. There
was no garbage collection where they lived, and Sam
Hughes had suggested they get a pig. Why bury good
scraps? Why not fatten up a pig? So a pig was to be
delivered the next day. Lawrence had mended the
fence down their lane, which enclosed several oak
trees. There the pig could argue with the squirrels over
the acorns. Miss Pru had supervised his chores with
great interest, and she had found she liked to lie on the
middle of the table in his room, where he had begun
to assemble the notes for his book. She made an excellent paper weight.

Sure enough, J.R. came by the next morning while
Bridget and her father were still at breakfast to
"carry" her to school. Acting businesslike, confident
and somewhat aloof, but with shimmers of excite-

ment, she thanked J.R. "That's very kind of you, but I really prefer to ride my Honda."

"Does Mrs. Smith know you're now referring to it as *your* Honda?" J.R. teased her, and Lawrence laughed. J.R. went on, "What if you run into another of our earthworms?"

Bridget's eyes were less confident, although she still declined to be carried to school. After all she was a Taylor, but her voice did squeak a little more.

Cheerfully, and not in the least put off, he told her he'd see her soon, and he left. She rode the Honda very carefully over the track, since her heart was in her mouth and she didn't want to risk jostling it. She saw no snakes.

When noon came, J.R. showed up in the lunch line at school. He sat by Bridget, having inveigled Mrs. Witmore to move down a seat. That way he could sit between them—a rose between two thorns, he claimed—with a sly grin at Bridget. He made the older woman laugh. He explained that one duty of the school board was to check out the school lunch now and then? Like a gourmand, he commented on each food as he tasted it.

As the kids filed back into class for the afternoon session, they asked Bridget all sorts of embarrassing questions. "We saw J.R. sitting by you in the cafeteria!" "Is he your boyfriend?" "Are you going to marry him?" "Is he a good kisser?" Worse luck, she felt herself blushing, which delighted the teasers.

She returned home that evening with her quickly darting eyes on the lookout for creepie-crawlies. She arrived safely, but she was really tired. Stress and fear are exhausting. Almost as soon as she got home, she had to go down to the pen with Lawrence and Miss Pru to inspect the pig. Pigs really didn't interest Bridget very much, but she was polite. The pig made rather rude noises and ignored her.

The rest of the week went well. The whole school soon knew that J.R. had lunch with Miss Taylor. Interest heightened when J.R. dropped in "to observe" her class on Thursday afternoon. Bridget was wearing a plaid shirtwaist that drew attention to her tiny waist and therefore to the womanly roundness above and below that waist. She didn't even know he was there until she turned from the blackboard to investigate the reason for the smothered giggling.

There sat J.R., squashed into a student desk, with his big tan hands folded primly on it. His sun-streaked hair was neatly combed, his knees hunched up and his booted feet in the aisle on either side of the desk. His eyes were guileless, his face betrayed no indication that he was out of place.

Chapter Three

Bridget had to brace her hand on the chalk tray to support her weakened knees. In order to help herself cope with her reaction to him, she tried to be very formal. "To what do we owe this pleasure, Mr. Winsome?"

The word "pleasure" is easily recognized, and the kids were all convinced that, in using it, Miss Taylor meant that she was pleased to see J.R. There was a spurt of knowledgeable snickering. After all, he'd been hanging around the school and even sat with her at lunch that one day.

J.R.'s crinkles deepened in a slight, tell-tale of delight at her discomfiture. He indicated the class was to proceed. It did, but J.R. had to bend a stern look now and again when sly, sideways, dancing-eyed giggles got a little out of hand.

Bridget had yard duty at recess, and J.R. tagged right along as she busily supervised the beejeebers out of those kids. There was a great deal of casual strolling past the couple by little girls, who hunched their shoulders and covered their grinning mouths with their hands if either adult looked their way.

J.R. allowed several of the boys to entice him into a pitch-and-catch ball game, and he threw the ball with deliberate ease, to show off for Bridget. He thought with some humor that he was no different from Little John lifting the mattresses.

In that time, she found he, too, used the questioning statement. He told Bridget that Little John, Bernice and he were going pecan hunting on Saturday morning? Would she like to go? The nuts would be handy for holiday baking. They'd take a picnic lunch and make a day of it. He and Little John would supply the lunch. She should just bring her pretty self?

With some calculation she inquired, "Little John's going?"

"Yeah—" his voice was a bit sour "—and Bernice."

"I had planned on going into San Antonio, to go to the library for Dad; but perhaps I could do that on Monday. Mrs. Moore will be back by then."

"Then you'll go?" He held his breath. When had he ever held his breath over a woman?

"I'd like to very much."

"Great! Wear some rough clothes, long pants, long sleeves and bring a sweater or a jacket. We'll have the lunch with us when we pick you up about...eight? Okay?"

"Fine."

But they had to postpone the picnic for a week. A "norther" blew in with cold rain and wild, tossing winds. The temperature "plummeted clear down" to thirty degrees for a day or two. The winds caused the temperamental electricity to fail. That's when the Taylors found out why there was a kerosene lamp, and the ancient refrigerator got an . . . automatic defrost.

With a cozy fire in the fireplace, and their snug Yankee clothing, the Taylors were quite comfortable. But the natives shivered and shook and exclaimed on the unusually cold fall weather.

So on Saturday, in the rain, Bridget went by bus to San Antonio as she'd originally planned. It was a pleasant ride. Another time she would sightsee. The Alamo was downtown. It was there that Bowie and Crockett had died helping Travis to fight Mexico for TEXAS's independence. They'd delayed the Mexicans, giving Sam Houston time to gather his army and later to defeat the Mexicans in the Battle of San Juacinto.

She considered how magnificent men really are. They are dreamers, romantic idealists, and willing to back their dreams with their lives. She wondered what they thought about—that handful of men at the Alamo one hundred fifty years ago—knowing they were doomed, but selling their lives for the dream for others with no gain for themselves at all. No wonder TEXAS cherished them so.

Bridget stopped on a bridge over the San Antonio River and looked down at the river walk. There were shops and restaurants crowded along the banks and, surprisingly, some lovely homes. She realized she would need time to explore the city, the Spanish Missions and the Hemisfair grounds. It would be an interesting winter.

Although others hurried through the gray day with its windy rain, Bridget strolled along, comfortable in her all-weather coat and hat. She window-shopped and one store especially caught her attention. It was filled with bargain items from Mexico. There were bright colorful materials, leather, carved wood, woven reeds, all in a marvelous jumble. It would take a month for a customer to see everything offered in the store. But a roughly woven woolen rug of rich browns and beiges with accents of black held her attention.

Bridget peeked at the cost and checked her wallet. She didn't quite have the price. She agonized over the rug, because it would look so cozy and warm in their bare living room. She sighed as she left the store to continue on toward the library, but she cast a last longing glance back at the rug.

At the library, Bridget presented her father's credentials and his list of books to the librarian, and she was directed to the research section and sat down there to wait until the books were sent from the stacks. Her eyes wandered around and saw...J.R.! He glanced up, nodded casually, and went back to his reading.

Bridget was astonished to see him, but then the librarian brought the books, and Bridget signed for them.

"Let me carry those, honey." It was J.R.

"Don't ca—"

"Miss Taylor...honey."

"What are you doing here?"

"I came to be with you. I stopped off to carry you into town and you'd already...you are an *eager* woman! And since I'd promised you lunch today..."

"Lunch?"

".You know," he explained. "The picnic. I didn't cancel lunch, just hunting pecans." He was helping her with her coat by then. "Where would you like to eat?" He picked up her books, escorted her from the library, and they walked outside into the rain.

She realized she'd have to eat somewhere so she thought for a minute and then asked, "At McDonalds? Do they have them down here?"

"Even in China. You ever tried TEXAS-Mexican food? Best there is."

"Yes. The first evening we were here."

"It's a gourmand's experience, right? We took plain old Mexican food and added the TEXAS touch. There's a good place just along the river down yonder."

By then they were approaching the jumbled store wherein lay "her" rug. Impulsively, she placed a hand on his arm to stop him as she said, "Do you have your car? May I ride home with you?"

"Why sure honey, that's why I'm here."

"And could you lend me one dollar and thirteen cents?"

"Sure."

"Good!" She was exuberant. "Then I can buy that rug!" And she laughed in delight.

They ate first. Bridget especially liked the beef enchiladas, and she practiced rolling the hot tortillas so the melting butter couldn't escape. He tried to convince her to call him J.R., but he finally settled for Jeremy. He liked the way it sounded with her husky, squeaky voice; and he watched the enticing way her lips moved as she said his name.

After they'd eaten, they walked along the deserted river walk in the fine rainy mist for quite a way. She exclaimed over the shops and the different kinds of stairways to the street, how pretty it all was and how beautifully planned.

As they walked along, Bridget realized that Jeremy too was well planned. He was marvelous. Not only in body, but in humor, in his ease with her, in his willingness to bend. It was very nice to walk beside him, to be with him as one half of a couple. It made her walk differently. She'd been strictly raised, a dedicated student and very involved in school activities. She'd had no time for the flirtations or affairs that others had experienced. The ones Bridget had heard about had been the disasters.

She'd never met a man like Jeremy Robert Winsome. With him she could be tempted to have an affair. She smiled. He hadn't even kissed her. He might be a zero. She rubbed a grin away with her hand. But she would soon know because he would probably kiss her that day. He'd come all the way to San Antonio to be with her, so he might very well kiss her.

They finally returned to the jumbled store for her rug. After Bridget had been very firm that she would pay for it, she ended up having to borrow ten dollars from Jeremy because she bought more than just the rug.

He was so amused watching her figure it all out. She bought the rug, a small blue pot for the Taylors' table and a big black pot to sit by the fireplace to hold kindling. Then, at a tiny hole-in-the-wall flower shop, she bought a pink flowering begonia to go in the blue pot. Jeremy insisted on buying the flowers.

They walked toward his car. Jeremy was carrying the rolled six-by-eight-foot rug over his shoulder and lugging that big black pot. Bridget carried the begonia in the blue table pot and all the books.

"J.R. Winsome, as we live and *breathe*!"

There were three nice-looking, TEXAS-tanned, exuberant men Jeremy's age. Jeremy laughed, put down the pot and shook their hands. The four men's greetings, and talk, overrode each other: "How you been, boy?" "What a long time!" "What you doing in town?" But mostly they were eyeing Bridget. Finally one nudged, "Come on, J.R., introduce us."

"Okay, okay, you guys. Settle down!" He named the three, then he said, quite emphatically, "This is *my* snow bird, Bridget Taylor."

"Snow bird, huh?" "Where you from, honey?" "J.R. making you carry all those books? Shame on him. Let me help you." "Here, let me carry that heavy old plant for you."

Jeremy complained that someone could help him, but they told him to hush, that he was interrupting, and hadn't his mama taught him better than that? With exclamations, questions and garbled conversation they all swept along in the gloomy rain to J.R.'s car where they deposited the books and Bridget's purchases.

Then they went to a nearby grill and spent an hour visiting and laughing as they carefully included Bridget with explanations. The three finally had to return to their offices. They left J.R. and Bridget on the street, with promises to meet at the fair, where J.R. had agreed that Gus would race.

Glancing back at the departing men, Bridget laughed. "I feel as if I've been in a friendly tornado! I have some questions."

"Fire away." He took her arm as they jumped a puddle in the gutter to cross the mist-swept street.

"Why did you call me a snow bird?"

"Honey, a snow bird is a Yankee farmer who comes south in a mobile home to sit out the northern winter in the TEXAS sunshine. We also call them Winter TEXANS."

"I'm not a farmer."

"No." He grinned down at her. "But you're a Yankee."

"I see. What's the fair and where is it?"

"That's a kind of Thanksgiving thing that started up after the Great Depression and keeps going. It's just an excuse for folks to get together and celebrate having survived, catch up on the gossip and show off what they've been doing. You'll like it."

"Ummm. And who or what is Gus?"

"He's my horse and his name is Pegasus. He is one *heck* of a runner."

"Pegasus and Cassius. Interesting names. It shows a thimbleful of imagination or romance that I wouldn't have guessed you had."

"Honey, I have a lively imagination." He slanted an appreciative look from her face to her ankles. "And I'm always willing to be romantic." He licked his upper lip and his crinkles deepened.

He might not be too hard to seduce. The thought made her blush and she laughed.

They eventually went back to the Mexican restaurant and selected a variety of food to share with Lawrence for supper. They drove back west in the rainy afternoon. It was so cozy in the car, and Bridget was electrically aware of Jeremy. She allowed herself glances at him as he drove. What would he say if she suggested they find a hidden lane? The thought made her very lax-muscled with restless insides. A strange contrast that probably accounted for her uneven breathing and nervous fingers.

Lawrence had built a fire for Miss Pru, who was curled in a fluffy ball on the hearth. Without moving, the cat managed to oversee the laying of the new rug. Jeremy had to admit the rug looked exactly right in front of the fire. He noted that the nondescript clean curtains had been mended and were back in place. He was amazed how the cheap rug and the blue pot of pink flowers changed the bare room.

The three worked together setting out the supper. The conglomeration of unmatched dishes, glasses and jars was funny, but the blue-potted begonia gave the round oak table flair. The rooms no longer looked poor, maybe a little eccentric, but not poor.

After they had eaten and cleared away, they pulled the lumpy brown couch over in front of the hearth and carried their cups of tea into the living room. There was no TV, but the radio played oldies but goodies. It felt very nice to sit by the fire with the rain still sounding on the tin roof.

After Lawrence drank the spiced tea, he excused himself, winning a smile from Jeremy. Lawrence said he thought he would thumb through some of the books they'd brought back. Bridget grinned, knowing he was itching to get his hands on those books.

So she had Jeremy alone and he would kiss her. He started to put another log on the fire. They could sit around talking forever! "No," she said. "Let it burn down. It's time for you to go."

"Al-*ready*?"

"Yes. It's been a wonderful day." She smiled at him. "Thank you for bringing me home. I love our new rug and the pots...oh!" She jumped up, and dropped a rather ruffled cat back onto the sofa. She went into her room and returned with his ten dollars.

He riffled through the bills. "Uh, there's *just* ten dollars here." Jeremy was serious. "There's the interest."

What had she gotten herself into? Cautiously she inquired, "Interest?"

"Yes." He rose from the sofa, moved to her, took her into his strong arms—and kissed her cross-eyed.

It was everything she'd ever dreamed a kiss could be. An affair. Yes. She gasped, not too clear-headed and murmured, "Is that supposed to be the...interest?" Even in her condition, she knew she sounded stupid.

"Well, it surely is interesting, but that's a Yankee dime. Now you had to know that, being a Yankee and all. During The War all those Yankee men came down here and told our ladies that very thing. Kisses are Yankee dimes."

"I never heard of it." She lay in his arms waiting for another...dime.

"Miss Taylor, honey, I've had a great day. I liked spending it with you. Don't forget next Saturday now, you hear?"

He wouldn't come to see her for a week?

"Good night." Jeremy smiled down at her as he released her slowly. She didn't help. He opened the door, put on his Stetson and again said, "Good night." It was he who closed the door between them, and she leaned against it because her knees were ruined. An affair. She was only going to be around long enough for a nicely full-blown affair, then she'd leave this land, go home and never see any of these people again. A good safe discreet affair.

By Monday all lingering signs of the norther had blown away and it was a pretty day. The natives thought it was still cold, but to Yankees it was only sweater weather. Bridget took the blue table pot down to the Smith store.

"Well, hello there, honey." Mrs. Smith returned her greeting, glad to see her.

"I haven't thanked you for the wood."

"The wood?" Mrs. Smith's face was blank.

"Jeremy brought it over last week and he said..."

"J.R. delivered wood?"

"Ummm. He said you told him it was just going begging, and I'd be doing a kindness to take it off your hands. Is there a charge? Did he pay you for it?"

"No."

"Then it's okay?"

"Absolutely." Mrs. Smith knew nothing about a load of wood and she could hardly wait to mention the matter to J.R.

"The wood's certainly nice to have, and Miss Pru especially is grateful. Oh, she has a caller…serenading her."

"Big Red, I'll bet. He gets to her first every time. He must keep close track of her whereabouts. He's a big old red tom, battle-torn and mean, but she adores him."

"That's the one. Have you see Little John?"

"Why'd you ask?"

"No reason." She'd turned away to finger some material as she explained, "I just wondered what happened to those dogs."

So Mrs. Smith assumed Bridget was interested in Little John. She showed Bridget some mill ends. These were lengths of woolen material printed perhaps a bit off, or soiled by the machinery or flawed. The prices were very reasonable. Bridget bought two lengths to send to her mother for skirts. And she coveted all the rest.

Mrs. Smith mentioned, as if it was an afterthought, that the Winsomes owned the mill, and the wool was mostly from their own sheep. Then she helped Bridget to match the blue pot with blue paint.

small, twisted, rough-barked mesquite trees. With great interest, Bridget walked around the patch and squatted down to peer along the little trails to see how the cactus grew in the stony ground which was so different from anything in Indiana.

The sound was very like the first chuff of a steam engine.

In some surprise, she turned her head and looked over her shoulder at the biggest, blackest, red-eyed bull she'd ever seen! Actually, it was the first one she had ever encountered, but she'd never realized they could be so large.

Bridget skinned up a tree and tried from it to figure out what route she'd taken through all that cactus in order to have gotten up in that particular mesquite. The bull seemed equally surprised by her move. She settled a trifle more securely on her branch to wait for the bull to go back over the hill and forget about her.

The bull bellowed, making Bridget clutch the tree. He was unbelievably loud! He snorted and pawed the ground, he swung his head and pranced around, and he was absolutely magnificent.

Her tree wasn't very tall, but when she realized he wouldn't come through the cactus, her heart gradually released its stranglehold on her windpipe and sank back down into place. She wondered how long she'd be there.

"When handed a lemon, make lemonade," as one of the clever, newspaper advice columnists said. So Bridget adjusted her position, got out her sketch book and began doing quick, rough sketches of the bull, which gradually became better.

When the sun was directly overhead, she ate half her sandwich, saving the rest in case she was still there, heaven forbid, for supper. She drank sparingly of the water. The bull never lost interest. He treated her to an occasional bellow that never failed to impress her. She continued to draw. It had never before occurred to her that she'd wanted to learn to draw a bull.

When she became too cramped, she very carefully stood up on her branch and tried to figure out a route through the cactus to the fence, but there was no way to go in that direction. The prickly cactus was like a bramble bush. If she got away, it would have to be back into the field and around the outside of that big patch of cactus, then back to the fence and out between the strands of barbed wire.

She had just settled down again, after stretching, when she heard the creak of leather, the jingle of a bridle and the muffled sound of a horse's hooves thudding up along the fence line. She turned so eagerly that she almost lost her balance, and the bull bellowed.

Of course, the rider was Jeremy.

Chapter Four

Jeremy told her in a reasonable voice, "Honey, you've got to quit teasing my bull!"

"Teasing!" Bridget couldn't believe he'd said that.

"He's been bellowing for two hours. If you're not teasing him, what are you doing sitting there in that tree just out of reach?"

She replied with fine sarcasm, "I'm sitting here learning to draw a bull!"

"Oh. Well. Then you don't need me." He lifted the reins and turned the horse's head as the dog Cassius came up to sit and watch.

"Jeremy!" She was very, very patient.

"Yeah, honey?" He tilted his head back to look at her from under the brim of his hat.

"You can't just go away and leave me here."

He turned back and stepped down from his horse with a beautiful, effortless flow of muscle. He moved to lean on a fencepost. "Did you happen to notice this fence was different from the others? Posts closer. Five strands of barbed wire?" He pronounced barbed as bobbed. "Wasn't that a hint that something was being kept in . . . or out?"

"I suppose."

"Now Casanova there. . ." He pointed with his chin.

"Casanova?"

"Yeah. He's not the faithful sort at all, and he's got enough to mull over in his wicked little brain without some luscious human female thinking he's Minotaur and wanting to be a virgin sacrifice."

"I *don't* want to be a virgin—"

"Good."

"—sacrifice."

"Oh." He surveyed her situation. "Are you waiting for a Hero then?"

"Yes, send for Little John."

He moved impatiently. "You've just got to give up on Little John. He's going to marry Bernice just as soon as she gets over me."

She gingerly shifted her position. "One of the ninety-eight percent, hmm?"

"Yeah." He sighed gustily. "It's something they all have to go through . . . like chicken pox. When they catch a dose of me young, they get over me in a reasonable time. Bernice was late with her case of me. When you catch me, honey, you're going to get a chronic case you'll never get over, because I'm going to *encourage* you."

"You've never encouraged any of the ninety-eight percent?"

He shook his head in a virtuous manner. "Nary a one." He sighed, took out a sack of tobacco and a paper to start making a cigarette. "I hate rolling my own, but when you're born in TEXAS, your parents have to swear you'll always roll your own."

"I've seen other Texans smoking commercial cigarettes."

"TEXANS, all caps remember; and anyone you see smoking tailor-mades isn't native. He's an infiltrating Yankee." As she laughed, he went on, "Anyway, rolling your own is part of the cowboy image, like squinting, looking off into the distance, wearing string ties and saying, 'yep.' Spurs are for the 'clink' sound. Gus would get so cranky if I actually used them."

She grinned, then she pleaded, "Jeremy, do something! Come get me out of here."

"Me? Come in there? Heck no! Just get on down out of that tree you're in and come on out."

"I can't. That bull scares me. I'm afraid he'll chase me."

"Well, he probably *will*. Can't you see how bored he is? No lady-cows around, nothing interesting to do. If you were a cat—the bull, on a rug—the field, and a mouse—you—ran across your rug, you'd chase it, wouldn't you?"

She wailed, "Jeremy!"

He wasn't in the least bit of hurry. He squinted at her. "Honey, did you leave anyone pining for you up there in Indian-er?"

"No!" She was becoming irritated.

"That's nice. What will you give me if I distract old Casanova?"

"My personal check for one million dollars."

J.R. scoffed. "Money! I don't need *money*!"

"What, then?" A nice lick of sensation curled around inside of her. He would say he wanted her, and she would simply have to agree, she'd have no choice.

"A kiss. A nice big squishy one. All rescued maidens in distress kiss their rescuer. It's the *rule*."

Disgruntled she replied, "That's not true."

He nodded definitely, and spaced his words: "Yes . . . it . . . is."

"No. They give the rescuer a scarf, which he then ties around his arm."

He started to get back on the horse.

"Jeremy!"

"Yeah, honey?"

"All right."

"A kiss, huh?"

"A . . . kiss."

Jeremy turned to his horse. "All right, Gus . . ."

"Gus? That's the horse, Pegasus? The *racer*?"

"Well now, honey, even you can see I can't hardly call him Peg!"

She burst out laughing. "That's Gus?"

Jeremy turned back to the horse and commented, "She just don't hardly sound respectful, do she." And the horse blew through loose lips.

Bridget said, "Send the dog to chase the bull away."

Very patiently Jeremy explained, "Cassius isn't a bull dog, he's a snake dog, I've told you that." Then he turned back to the horse and, gesturing, said,

"Gus, trot down yonder to those trees and look into them real curious like?"

Whether the horse actually understood the words or was really following the hand signals, Bridget didn't know. The horse lifted his head and looked toward the trees in question, then he looked back at J.R. with a you've-got-to-be-kidding-me expression.

"Go *on*!" It was a command that time.

The horse lowered his head and went off like an indifferent hunting dog on an obscure scent. She'd never seen a horse do that, but then she'd never seen very many horses. Sure enough, he went down to the trees and stretched his neck up to stare into them.

The bull watched alertly, snorting, and then he *had* to go look, too, trotting with remarkable grace, considering his bulk.

J.R. hissed, *"Now!"*

Bridget skinned out of the tree and flung herself along the only reasonable path through the cactus, fled around the perimeter, and then dived between the barbed wire—held apart between J.R.'s foot and one hand.

The bull tore back, bellowing, and Bridget grabbed Jeremy with a shriek. J.R. laughed, held her close with one arm and with the other hand waved his hat at the bull as he yelled, "HAAH!" The bull pulled up short of the fence, snorting, pawing, bellowing. He was e-nor-mous! Then he trotted around, showing off how beautiful he was, shaking his horns, threatening to come through the fence.

Cassius had sat and watched the whole procedure with forbearance. His nose skimming the weeds, Gus ambled back and stopped beside them. Bridget gingerly picked up his head and kissed the horse's soft nose.

"What are you doing?"

"I've just kissed my rescuer."

"Oh, hell!" J.R. flung his hat at the ground. Bridget laughed, her eyes dancing as she rubbed and stretched the kinks from her body, cramped from sitting so long in that tree. J.R. stood with his hands on his hips, feet apart, as he watched her with narrowed eyes.

Curiously, she asked, "How did you happen to come by?"

"I told you. I heard the bull complaining."

"He wasn't complaining, he was *threatening* me."

"He wouldn't hurt a fly...that we know of. Of course, no one goes in there and runs around on the ground to find out, him being bigger and all. The only human we know antagonizes him is the veterinarian."

"With shots?"

"We-e-ll, not the kind you're thinking about. We had the vet out to administer artificial insemination to a couple of dairy cows, and Casanova got loose and rammed in the side of the vet's pickup!"

"Did he really?"

"Yep. Did you catch that 'yep'?" He watched as she moved her stiff body, and his eyes darkened. "You owe me a kiss."

"I do not. Gus rescued me."

"I was the strategist—the brains. You owe me, honey." He moved closer.

Pushing back her hair, looking utterly lovely, she turned right into his arms. Her lips were parted to sass him, and he kissed her before she could say a word. He slowly wrapped his arms around her and pulled her sweet softness tightly to his own hard body, as he continued to kiss her.

She gave a token resistance but was distracted by the strange, delicious flickering up the middle of her body. She was kissing him back. Her hands slid up his arms to the back of his head, and she blushed.

That only made her look more charming to J.R., when he finally lifted his head and gazed down at her. She clung there, with her arms around his neck, her eyes serious, face blushing, her mouth invitingly close. Her blush deepened.

So he kissed her again. Long and marvelously. As he finally loosened his hold, he had to set her away from him. She stumbled, and he steadied her. He explained, "I took two, so I owe you a rescue." His words were light, but his face was deadly serious. The crinkles around his eyes were so solemn that there were untanned lines fanning out from his eyes. His blue-green eyes were dark behind his sun-bleached lashes. His breathing had quickened and his hands were not quite steady. "Do you know your way home?"

"Ummmm." Her nod was a little loose since she was still thinking about kissing.

"Can you get back to your place all right? I can't take the time to go with you now, honey. Will you be all right? Or do you want to come with me? I could get you home from my place later?"

"No." She smiled so sweetly that she disturbed him further. "I'll be all right."

"Cassius." He turned briefly to the dog. "You go with her and take care of her. Guard her. Hear me?"

"No." It wasn't the dog who replied, but Bridget who objected. She didn't like dogs.

"Honey, if you're bound and determined to walk around on the ground, you need Cassius."

"Dogs scare me, and if Cassius was slinking along beside me all the time, I'd be nervous."

"You won't be nervous with Cassius."

"Cassius helped *kill* Caesar! How do I know this Cassius isn't in league with the snakes?"

"Trust him."

"No."

"Whether or not you agree, he's going to stay with you, and if you or your daddy walk around on the ground, Cassius is going along." He tilted up her face and gave her a no-nonsense look. "Cross this field to that fence, follow its line to the burned-out house on the river, you'll find the steps down to the bridge to cross there, then go left two fields and you'll see your house." He still held her head between his hands and he said softly in his deep voice, "Although I owe you a rescue, take care of yourself, hear?"

"Yes, sir."

"That's the way I like to hear you talk, honey." He gave her a swift kiss, then he told her matter-of-factly, "That's not a real kiss, so it's free." And he smiled at her.

She thought they might very well have an affair.

Cassius whined, moved his front feet and pulled his ears down in a pleading way. J.R. squatted on his heels to rub the dog's head and shoulders, but he repeated his command. He rose, stepped into the saddle, and Cassius was obviously appalled. Jeremy spoke gently but firmly to the dog, he looked a long intense time at Bridget, then turned Gus and rode off.

Bridget and the dog stood there in the afternoon sunshine and watched J.R. ride away. She'd never seen a horse walk like that—with its head along the brush. Then the dog whined so faintly, she thought it sounded like a smothered sob. She knelt down and astonished them both by hugging the dog to comfort him.

Bridget finally met Bernice the next day. It was another pretty day. The meeting started well enough. Bernice came with Little John. They got out of a rusty, nondescript pickup that was as tacky as his station wagon. Bernice had a nice friendly smile for Bridget, because Mrs. Smith had told her Bridget favored Little John.

The conversation was typical, as among people just meeting: "How do you like it here?" "Just fine." "How long are you staying?" But all along they were sizing each other up. Then Lawrence came out on the porch to say hello, and Bernice turned on a blinding smile for his benefit.

On being introduced, Bernice said, "Well, hel-lo! I'd heard Bridget was here with her daddy. If I'd known a daddy looked like you, I wouldn't have worn this tacky old outfit." Blond, voluptuous and blue-eyed, Bernice was entirely confident she'd look stunning in a potato sack. Lawrence smiled.

Bridget watched amazed as Bernice simpered and preened. Annoyed with Bernice, Bridget studied her father to see if he realized Bernice was flirting with him. He was relaxed, leaning against a porch post, his hands in his pockets, amused and enjoying Bernice's performance.

Bridget had always thought he looked like a father. She was astonished to suddenly see him as a still-young, good-looking, virile, forty-six-year-old male!

There was a whole conversation going on between the other three. Bridget looked at each one, as he or she spoke, but her own thoughts whirled on.

It was then that Bridget noticed how her father was handling Bernice's blatant behavior: calmly and with a practiced kindliness. One seldom expects a parent to be smooth or sophisticated. She wondered if her mother realized he was. But then he had been teaching female students the same age as Bernice for a long time. He'd had practise!

Did her mother realize that other women saw her husband...as a *man*? It was a shocking thought. Her father was a very attractive man.

Bridget tuned in on the conversation as her-father-the-stranger spoke to Bernice. "Sam Hughes told me that your dad enjoys chess. I'm to meet him when he returns home."

"Oh, marvelous!" Bernice said. "He'll be back this Thursday. Dad's kind of an old fuddy-duddy, but he's sweet."

Bridget resisted giving an explosive sigh at Bernice's silliness and glanced at Little John only to see that he watched Bernice with fond, indulgent eyes. She thought maybe Jeremy was right. Little John really did love Bernice. There's no accounting for taste.

About that time, Cassius slinked around the corner of the house and sat quietly at Bridget's side. Bernice's eyes widened in surprise. "Oh! Is J.R. here?"

"No," Bridget replied.

"Then what's his dog doing here?" she demanded.

"Jeremy says he's a good snake dog, and since we insist on walking around on the ground, he left the dog to walk with us."

In shock, Bernice exclaimed, "Cassius would never leave J.R.!"

Bridget didn't know how to reply since obviously the dog wasn't with Jeremy but with her. Then Miss Pru pushed open the screen and ambled out to see what was going on.

Bernice gasped, "That's Miss Pru!"

"Yes," Bridget admitted.

Bernice turned an indignant, belligerent look on Bridget-the-interloper. If they'd been inside the house, friendship would have flown right out the window.

Bridget did invite them in for tea, but Bernice declined coldly, saying they had to leave. That information surprised Little John as he'd already started toward the porch. Bernice thawed briefly to tell Lawrence goodbye. Then she stood straight and cold as Little John said they'd see Bridget on Saturday for the pecan hunt. She agreed, and they left.

The Taylors watched the rusty pickup drive away with surprising smoothness. Bridget bit out, "What a witch!"

Lawrence grinned. "No, just a late bloomer. Give her a little time." Then he put a hand on his daughter's shoulder and said, "Bridget, I believe Little John cares for her."

"I think so, too."

Like Mrs. Smith, Lawrence mistakenly thought Bridget might be interested in Little John. "It doesn't bother you?"

"Not at all."

"Good."

Later, Bridget and Cassius went to the store to get some blue material that she could stuff for cheerful sofa pillows. Mrs. Smith was outside, supervising the sinking of six telephone poles. Bridget noted the rolls of snow fencing ready nearby.

The older lady paused in her unneeded supervision to frown a smile at Bridget and threaten her, "If this doesn't work, you're going to carry that fencing to Indiana on your *back*!"

Bridget promised, "It'll work. You'll love me for suggesting it; and when I'm gone, you'll tell everyone, 'Those Yankees are smart!'"

"Humph! I'd have thought of it, if we had any use for that sort of fencing down here in all this glorious TEXAS sunshine." They grinned at each other before Mrs. Smith asked, "What's Cassius doing with you?"

"Jeremy made him stay."

"Oh?" Mrs. Smith raised exceedingly alert eyebrows and waited pointedly for more information.

Bridget sighed. "Because I insist on 'walking around on the ground.' I'd like to know where else I'm supposed to walk!"

Mrs. Smith was so bemused by the fact that J.R. would make Cassius stay with Bridget that she neglected the supervision. Oddly, the work went right ahead.

Bridget added thoughtfully, "Do you know, I think Little John likes Bernice."

"Why do you think that?"

"I watched him look at her."

"So you've met Bernice."

Bridget rolled her eyes. "What a *witch*!"

Mrs. Smith laughed. "Give her time."

"You're the third person to say that. I can't see how time is going to help her."

"Who were the other two?"

She flung out a hand. "My dad and Jeremy."

It was very interesting to Mrs. Smith that J.R. had discussed Bernice and Little John in that manner with Bridget, and she wondered how and why that subject had come into the conversation. "Wait and see. She'll shape up, and you'll end up liking her."

"That's not possible."

"Come along," Mrs. Smith said with a grin. "I've got something for you." She turned to the men, shouted that she'd be gone for a couple of minutes and could they spare her for that time? They replied that they would surely try.

Mrs. Smith led Bridget around to the back of the building where she indicated some plants she had for her. There were pots of parsley, rosemary, thyme and mint. All vigorous, healthy plants. Bridget was so touched that she hugged the startled woman. Then she teased that she was astonished TEXANS knew about herbs. She thought they just put chili peppers in everything and ignored the other seasonings.

Mrs. Smith looked at Bridget with a tiny smile, reached into the potting shed slowly and brought out the fifth pot. A gorgeous jalapena pepper plant! Bridget laughed until she had to wipe her eyes, and Mrs. Smith laughed with her.

She told Bridget in precise detail how to care for the plants, then, apparently not trusting Bridget, she used a marking pen to write those instructions on each pot. She told Bridget that Little John would deliver them in the next day or so. Bridget had to smile. Poor Little John, the errand boy.

Bridget instructed Cassius to wait outside, and he sat obediently by the door while she went into the store with Mrs. Smith. Bridget chose a portable sewing machine to rent for a month, which Little John would deliver with the plants. The material for the pillows and the stuffing didn't take long to choose. However, Mrs. Smith was essentially a lonely woman, who didn't give her friendship easily; so Bridget chatted patiently and didn't mind being instructed minutely in pillow making.

Bridget also selected some more of the mill ends. She needed the lighter Southern wool for skirts and jackets if she was going to teach. She loved the colors and took pleasure in matching and contrasting the pieces she'd chosen.

When Bridget finally left the store, Mrs. Smith stood for a serious minute or two watching after the young woman and Cassius as they walked off down the road. Then she roused herself and hurried back to her neglected supervising.

It wasn't Little John who delivered the plants on Thursday morning, it was Jeremy. Bridget had just finished scrubbing the kitchen floor on her hands and knees, and when she saw Jeremy she could have just died.

She was barefooted, her hair, once pinned up out of the way, was now partly tumbled down. She wore no makeup, and she had on an old Indiana University T-shirt and cutoffs. She was not Affair Tempting Material at all! She blushed and had no inkling what an enchanting picture she made. Jeremy looked up at her from where he squatted, petting Cassius. She smiled shyly, and he rose as he returned her smile, charmed by her.

"Uh...has Mrs. Smith adopted you, too?" she asked.

"No. Fortunately. But she did say that Little John was going to deliver those plants and a sewing machine to you. I figure the less you see of him the quicker you'll get over him, so I volunteered."

"That was nice of you."

He slanted a look around, leaned over and kissed her. She gasped. He said, "Now you only owe me nine."

"How could I owe you ten, or now, nine kisses? You didn't rescue me, and I haven't borrowed any more money from you."

"Well, you went to the store with Cassius, so I figure he saved you from at least five snakes going and the same five coming back."

"I didn't see even one!"

"See how good he is?"

Cassius pushed his head under and against Jeremy's hand, and he petted the dog with absent-minded gentleness as he watched Bridget. She was laughing, her hands to her head, trying to tidy her hair. He looked down her graceful, lusciously rounded body, with the T-shirt damp with sweat and clinging to her, and his body stirred.

He glanced around again, then reach out, drew her to him and kissed her thoroughly, in spite of her soft protests. But it thrilled him when she said she was so dirty! So, it wasn't his kisses she protested. He chuckled and was very pleased. He tried to hold her, but she pushed away, feeling terribly embarrassed.

She helped him bring the plants to the porch and thought they looked elegant grouped against the wall. She made Jeremy admire the material for the sofa pillows and then the blue-painted chairs. He did this sincerely and with some surprise. "You're going to sew those?" His mother couldn't sew on a button.

The blue of the sofa pillows was interrupted only by a tiny dot of pinkish orange here and there in the pattern, which picked up the pink of the begonia across the room in the blue pot on the table. It was nice, he thought, really very nice. He looked around again, seeing how just those touches Bridget had added made the poor bare room now seem warm and welcoming.

Then he smiled, because above the fireplace was a charcoal drawing of a belligerent, arrogant, magnificent black bull, standing in challenge. She'd drawn it from her sketches. "Oh, honey, that is good!"

"I had plenty of time to study him." She drawled it out with such exaggerated drollness that she made him grin.

"I want it. Put a price on it."

"When we go home next spring, I'll give it to you." She was surprised when, at her words, he snapped his head around and a frown briefly shadowed his face as he looked at her very seriously.

Before he left he said she was needed the next day to substitute in the first grade and would she be available? She said, "Of course."

He smiled at her as he replied, "Those lucky little kids."

Chapter Five

There was a light fog on Friday, and the temperature was "clear down" to about forty-eight degrees. Bridget chose a light blue wool suit for her day at school. With her all-weather coat and hat, she was quite comfortable riding her Honda, followed by Cassius who courteously saw her to the school door. She told the dog to "go home," and he left. Then she wondered where he would go? To Jeremy's or to the Taylor house?

She went into the building where she was greeted cheerfully and directed to the correct room. The lesson plans were in the second drawer. Her first-grade class filed in, and their grins revealed most of them were minus their two front teeth, and none of them looked old enough to be in school.

Bridget stood, waiting for them to settle down so she could introduce herself, when a little boy said slyly, "'Lo, Miss Taylor, honey," just like Jeremy did. The whole class was hit with the giggles except for one glowering little feminine face. Another of the ninety-eight percent who found Jeremy irresistible? Bridget had to laugh. There's nothing more infectious than little kids' laughter.

In turn, the kids stood up and told her their names. Rita was the glaring one. Some were rather difficult to understand because they were snaggle-toothed. Bridget explained her problem understanding them by telling them where she lived. She pointed out Indiana on the pull-down map. Then she showed them their town in TEXAS. She said her way of speaking was a little different, and they must be patient with her.

It was a light-hearted, charming day. They called her "Mith Taylor, honey" all day, and she finally gave up trying for just "Mith Taylor." By lunchtime, the sun was beating down, and by two that afternoon, Bridget was slowly baking in her woolen suit. That day taught her to dress so she could peel off layers.

When school was over, and Bridget had tidied the room, she found Cassius waiting for her by the Honda. How had he known to come back? He trotted patiently beside her going home. Fortunately, he didn't leave the track to investigate anything. Since he was a "snake" dog, it would have made her nervous if he'd gone off chasing anything.

She rode the scooter into the yard to find her father, Bernice and Mr. Peters on the porch. Her dad had brought out two of the blue chairs to augment the wicker porch chairs, and there was some beer on the wicker table. Briefly Bridget's eyes took pleasure in seeing the bright blue of the chairs with the greyed-brick-red wicker, the mustard door and Mrs. Smith's green plants against the weathered siding.

Bridget greeted her father and Bernice, who introduced her father. Bridget almost went "boing" with shock! The "old fuddy-duddy" was a handsome man! He was Lawrence's age, and the same height, but somewhat stockier. He looked as if he'd been stood out in the rain and rusted. His hair, eyebrows, lashes and freckles were all that color. His eyes were dark blue and alive! His name was Mark Peters, and he was a widower.

"No one has ever called you Rusty?" Bridget smiled.

"Not after I objected a time or two." His voice was attractive, and his eyes glinted with humor. "Did you catch cold with our chilling morning?" He referred to her foggy voice.

Lawrence explained how she'd been a cheerleader and, single-voiced, tried to bring her school teams out of the basement. Then he added to Bridget, "I see Cassius found you."

"So he was here. I told him to go home and he left, then I wondered where he'd go."

Bernice frowned at that and impatiently tossed back her blond hair.

Mark asked lazily, "That's J.R.'s dog, isn't it?" When they agreed, he tilted his head and considered Bridget in penetrating glances. "He got you staked out?" His deep voice was soft.

She replied, "We've only been here a short time. J.R. left the dog with us because we insist on walking around on the ground. He's just being nice."

Mark's look was speculative and his voice still soft. "It would be very easy to be nice to you."

Bridget was uncomfortable with the conversation, so Lawrence moved their talk to general topics. Bridget caught several glimpses of humor in Bernice, who was acting reasonably normal, with the "old fuddy-duddy" there. Her humor was mostly for Lawrence, though some was indulgently for her own father, but there was absolutely nothing for Bridget. While Bernice seemed to believe Bridget didn't exist, Mark was very aware of her.

If she didn't know Jeremy, or if she'd been fifteen years older, it would have been fun and very interesting to have flirted with Mark. To have just enjoyed his flirting, but she'd met Jeremy, and she was too young for Mark.

Mark and Bernice stayed for supper, inspected the pig, and finally left about ten o'clock. The Taylors had promised they would have Sunday dinner with them at The Club. There was talk about a weekend on Padre Island, and Mark held Bridget's hand only a shade too long as they said good-night.

Saturday morning was chilly, but the sun came up with confidence. It promised to be another pretty day...which could get monotonous. How can anyone talk about the weather when it's always nice? Bridget's mother wrote the bare Indiana trees had been scratching the bellies of the clouds for a week, and what was the sun really like?

Saturday was the day of the postponed pecan hunting and picnic. As directed, Bridget dressed in a long-
sleeved, cotton shirt of a printed red bandanna pattern. She wore jeans and a blue jean jacket. She automatically wore boots, because in Indiana, even in
summer, the ground seldom dried out enough to wear
canvas shoes or sandals to hike in a wooded area.

Bridget and Cassius were waiting on the porch when
the others arrived just before eight. Little John was
driving a rusty four-wheel drive. Bernice sat between
the two men in the front seat. They exchanged greetings. With a big grin, Jeremy started to get out of the
car. Bernice slid out right behind him, and she said
firmly, "J.R. and I will sit in the back."

"No, no," Bridget protested, already opening the
back door. "Stay right where you are. Cassius and I
will sit in back." She solved the problem by doing just
that.

Bernice was pleased with the arrangement and sat
close to Jeremy, saying, "Have you enough room to
drive, Little John?"

"More than adequate." He cast her a droll glance.

Then Bernice wiggled her shoulder and said, "Put
your arm up, J.R. Your shoulders are too wide."

J.R. slowly swung his left arm over Bernice's head,
turning his back against the door, so that now Bernice had more than adequate room. J.R. tipped his
head forward so that, from under the brim of his
Stetson, he could slant a hilarious grin back at Bridget.

She had to cough a little to keep from giggling.
Cassius whined softly to attract Jeremy's attention,

and J.R. dropped his arm over the back of the seat to fondle the dog's head...and comfortably rest his forearm on Bridget's knees.

"How many cars do you have, Little John?" Bridget asked. "This is the third one I've seen you drive."

"Only six...no, seven since I've got that VW."

"Is it new?"

J.R. laughed. "No, it looks just like all the rest: tacky."

Bridget offered, "I'll help you paint them."

Little John replied, "That's sweet of you, but they're supposed to look this way. I use them in my job."

"Not, I take it, as errand boy for Mrs. Smith?"

His chin lowered. "No," he said, smiling at her in the rearview mirror.

It was J.R. who explained. "We have a tough time down here with smugglers bringing stuff in from Mexico. They don't expect anything like Little John. He putts along in his beat-up old cars, and they know they can get away. They put on the gas, thumbing their noses, and Little John gives chase. The smugglers floor it, rocking along, ninety miles an hour, and Little John zooms up.

"The smuggler watches that old car catching up that fast, and he naturally assumes that *his* car is suddenly standing still! So he gets out to see if his motor dropped out...when he's still going ninety! Little John catches lots of smugglers that way." He grinned. "So then the word goes out, 'For Pete's sake, watch out for a rusty, beat-up old car! It's hiding some wild kind of engine and a very nasty, hard-nosed marshal!' We've got a lot of old, beat-up, rusty cars gasping along the roads around here that are now treated with great respect. Lately, we don't have very many smugglers come through here. They think all those rusty old cars hold lawmen!"

"Is this another 'new boy' joke?" Bridget asked.

Little John replied, "Not entirely."

They left the paved road. In Indiana it would be called a hard road. They eased along the two-rutted, rocky track. Here and there, along the way, the road went under a stream, which they forded. Bridget was enthralled. The water was clear, shallow, running busily along, gurgling over rounded stones and gravel.

They finally turned into and drove along in one stream. They went under an old, concrete bridge that supported railroad tracks. Little John explained, "We're going to a secret place where there's a natural grove of pecan trees."

Bridget asked curiously, "Bernice, how long have you lived in this area?"

"All my life." She was flippantly dismissive. Then, equally curious, she was forced to ask, "Why?"

"Well, last night your father spoke of 'the natives,' so I thought perhaps you were rather new here."

"My daddy inherited our place about twenty-five years ago? He came here then and met my mama and married her."

"But your father still doesn't feel as if he belongs here?" Bridget questioned.

"We have a great deal of property all over the country. My daddy and mama used to travel most of the time. I went to boarding school in San Antonio."

"I see." Bridget thought of her own close family and felt sympathy for the lonely child, Bernice.

The sympathy must have come faintly into Bridget's "I see," and that annoyed Bernice. "Why do you say 'father' instead of 'daddy'? It sounds so formal: Faw-thar," she mocked.

"I don't know. I guess because where I live, most of us say dad or father. I think daddy sounds warm and loving. But habit's hard to break."

J.R. looked back at her and his eyes danced. "And you leave out the 'r' in warsh."

"Wash doesn't have an *r*." She grinned at him.

"Little John, say w-a-s-h."

"Warsh."

"See?" As she laughed, he went on quickly, "And you say 'as' instead of 'like,' and you say 'win-dough' instead of 'win-dah.'" He shook his head. "Strange woman."

"I'm strange! Have you ever listened to the way you speak? You say 'jest' for 'just' and 'git' for 'get.' Don't any of you ever see a dictionary?"

"Honey, we don't need one! We all talk alike, and we understand one another entirely. Why should we get a Yankee book that corrupts the pronunciation of good TEXAS words?"

They arrived at the secret place and found two other cars there. The occupants of those cars busily threshed the trees with long poles, but they froze as the Scout halted.

Little John and J.R. nearly always wore guns. They climbed slowly out of the Scout, and Little John opened the back door of the car to let Cassius out of the back seat. The dog slinked to the ground and disappeared into the brush. Then Little John opened the back of his vehicle. Suddenly the threshers threw down their poles, abandoned their cloths and sacks, scrambled into the two cars, and roared away.

J.R. grinned. "Man alive! A guilty conscience gets them every time!" He narrowed his eyes. "Wonder how they found this place? It's not exactly on the beaten path. Ever see them before, Little John?"

"No. Don't think I ever did. Must have spotted the grove from the air and come in? They were sure off in a hustle. Left their poles and drop cloths."

"I'll send some of the boys over Monday to finish up."

Bridget was uncomfortable. "Who owns this land?"

J.R. told her, "Little John and I bought it about seven years ago with our graduation money from high school."

"Oh."

"Did you think we were trespassing too?"

"I didn't know."

"We really don't mind sharing with families who take the windfalls for themselves, but amateur commercial poachers are another thing entirely. They harm the trees, strip the grove and don't leave enough even for the squirrels. We'll have to prepare for them next fall, now they've found the grove."

"How?" She looked around the very isolated area.

"The grove is worth protecting. We hate to fence it because it would keep the casual gleaners away, and we don't mind them. And this is a pretty area for picnics. We'll have to figure out something.''

J.R. and Little John dug a pit in the side of a bank, lined it with stones and built a hardwood fire on top of the stones. While the fire burned down to coals, they tidied up after the trespassers. The poachers had harvested sufficient sacks of nuts so the foursome didn't gather more.

When the fire was ready, J.R. removed most of the coals from the now hot rocks. A rack was positioned and a large cut of beef was placed on it. The meat was covered with wet canvas, which in turn was covered with dirt. By noon the meat would melt in their mouths.

"Where do you want to go, Bernice?" J.R. smiled at her as he patted the dirt covering till it was firm.

Bernice replied eagerly, "The cave!"

"Good," he said to her, then called to Little John, "We'll meet you all at the cave about eleven?" And he took Bridget's hand and started walking away.

"Where are you all going?" Bernice was startled.

"We'll see you at the cave," J.R. replied with patient exaggeration.

Not even Bernice knew how to counter that. She went with Little John, but she felt crossed.

Jeremy and Bridget left the grove in the hollow and walked along the rocky ground where a faint path led through the gnarled trees, dried weeds and cactus. The sun was bright and Cassius was happy to be near J.R., who had captured Bridget's hand. She said, "The red bird's song here is slightly different. Do you know what it says?''

"I give up."

"No, not 'I give up.' Listen the next time you hear one. It says: 'Bernice Bernice Bernice—terrible terrible terrible'.''

J.R. chuckled. "When she marries Little John, and you two are dear friends, you'll have to figure out some other words for the bird's song."

"I won't have to strain my brain. It'll never happen."

"Just wait." He knew she wasn't convinced. As they walked along, he asked, "What's the problem, honey?''

She frowned at him in a chiding way. "Jeremy, you just must stop calling me 'honey.' '' And she told him about the snaggle-toothed first-graders calling her "Mith Taylor, honey" all the day before, "with one exception."

"That would be Rita." He liked it that the first-graders had copied him and that Bridget was really quite amused.

"Now how could you know it was Rita?"

"One day she told me that I wasn't to get married until she was just a little older, so I suspected she'd joined the, uh, ninety-eight-percent?" He looked at her and would have liked to simply stare. But what he really wanted was to make love to her. To distract himself, he asked again, "Tell me what's troubling you."

"How do you know I have a problem?"

"I can tell." He knew he would always know.

"Well," she began. "I'm probably wrong, but..."
And she told him she suspected Mark Peters was attracted to her, and that he was making all sorts of plans for the two families—Padre Island, the Big Bend country, Colorado skiing. "And while I want Dad to have the friendship, I don't want it to include me."

Quite cheerfully, Jeremy commented, "Sounds like that old man's really crowding you!" And she wasn't interested! he thought. Jeremy knew Mark. He could be a formidable rival. Jeremy told Bridget, "You're a lucky girl to have your Uncle Dudley-Do-Right here to your rescue—again. You will recall I owe you one rescue?" He was so pleased with the turn of events that he was hard put not to kiss her mindless. "Now—" he pretended to settle down to serious business "—here's the plan. Whenever any activity's suggested, you say, 'Oh that sounds like fun. Dad will be delighted. However I can't go. I've a date with that darling man, Jeremy Winsome!' You can vary that with handsome or clever or brilliant. You can most likely think of *endless*—"

"How about modest?" she asked helpfully.

He frowned thoughtfully. "I don't...think...so."

She clutched her hair in delight before she sobered. "You realize—" Then she stopped.

"Of course!" He put his arm around her shoulders. "If anyone asks me if I have a date for such and such, I'll say, 'Naturally.' Oh, honey—" he interrupted himself, as if just remembering "—there's a dance brewing for next Saturday. Go with me?"

"I'd like to, please."

"What are you doing tomorrow?" Now who was trying to box her in?

"Well, Mark has us going to The Club for dinner after church..."

His free hand made a calming gesture. "Leave everything to me. I have a secret weapon."

"What secret weapon?"

"If I told you, it wouldn't be secret, would it? You owe me a bunch of kisses. Give me a couple now and we'll see how many I can handle at a time."

She badly wanted to kiss him, to be kissed by him. One did ease into an affair, didn't one? "Are these the saved-from-the-snakes kisses?"

"Piling up. Cassius is doing a great job of it. Come here and pay your debts, or you could end up spending whole nights just kissing me."

She had to take a quick breath at the very thought of a whole night of kissing him. She reached, he helped, and the kiss was amazing. Her body was thrilled and excited, her mouth eager, and her fingers quickly tangled in his hair, knocking off his Stetson. She heard it hit the ground, then her ears buzzed and her head reeled, so she didn't hear anything else.

He released her abruptly and turned away, walking around as he shoved his hands deep into his pockets. He kicked at stones, then stood pushing his arms straight down and taking deep breaths. He cleared his throat, bent down and picked up his Stetson, and settled it back on his head. "Maybe just one at a time? Woman, you're dangerous!"

He was obviously aroused. Her mother had told her it was unkind to deliberately do that to a man, and she knew she should leave Jeremy alone. For now. It was nice to know he could be attracted. It would make seducing him easier if he helped, but for now she should distract him. She said, "Will there be round dancing next Saturday?"

He looked back at her over his shoulder. "Round dancing?"

"You know, as opposed to square dancing. It's an excellent description."

"Do you believe in Equal Rights and Women's Lib and all that stuff?"

"Absolutely!" Her head came up to sniff for battle. "What does round dancing have to do with Equal Rights."

"Let's have an affair."

He had actually suggested it! "I..." Her foggy voice didn't know what to say.

"If we have an affair, we'll know if we're compatible. You need to try me out." He looked guileless and noble. Sharing.

She hadn't really thought they'd begin an affair by...discussing it. She was silent as she considered the matter, stalling. "I do know a lot about you already."

"Tell me."

He picked up her hand, kissed it and then held it as they walked along, discussing their affair, for Pete's sake. She said, "You have a dreadful temper."

"Rigidly controlled."

"You're humorous, romantic..." she began.

He sighed gustily. "Lord, I sure try."

She finished, "As shown in the naming of Cassius, Pegasus and Casanova."

"Oh. That kind." He dismissed that kind.

"And you're loved by ninety-eight percent of the women."

"Good grief, you'll probably even tell that to our great-grandchildren!"

Grandchildren? She frowned as her tongue continued, "And unusually skilled at kissing."

"It has to be a natural talent. You're the first lady I ever kissed." He smiled an innocently wicked look, then he said, "I know about you too, honey. You're beautiful and I like the way you smell."

She could only remember him kissing her just after she'd finished scrubbing the floor.

"You're sweet to your family, and you all care about one another. You like kids. You make a house warm and welcoming, you're a good teacher at school and look how well you've taught me to kiss in just a couple of tries!"

She laughed.

"You draw good bulls. You're unusually talented, and your body drives me crazy. I want to make love to you. That's amazing when you consider you're just a rag, a bone and a hank of hair. You have to be a witch. Have you fooled me? Did I really like your kiss that well?" So he kissed her again to find out, and it about wrecked them both. He gave her a long serious look before he smiled and said, "This will take some concentrated investigation."

She couldn't reply. Although she couldn't manage any more conversation, she could kiss some more.

However, Jeremy didn't kiss her again. He gave her
some soft quick ones, but no real kisses. He'd said
something about a cave, and she stumbled along beside him. A cave would be a good place to begin their
affair.

Chapter Six

They reached the cave just after eleven. Little John and Bernice were already there. Bridget had hoped the other two would have gotten lost. She looked around dismally. Little John said, "See? It isn't a real cave. It only goes back about twenty feet. It was most likely carved out by the ancient seas. Legend claims it was an Indian council place. Makes you wonder, with all the places designated as Indian meeting places, they must have sat around visiting just a whole lot."

Bridget surfaced from her sensual daze as they moved around. She found an arrowhead and was pleased with it, but the others weren't terribly impressed. Jeremy told her, "I've a whole collection, all sizes. You'll have to see it."

She gave him a sly smile the others couldn't see as she said, "I thought it was etchings a man used to lure a woman to his apartment."

He tried not to smile. "Won't arrowheads do?"

Bernice watched their by-play thoughtfully. Then they all agreed they were starving and walked back to the car. The men lay a ground sheet under a thick quilt and tossed the women pillows for seats. They took the roast out of the pit and set it aside to rest before being sliced. The aroma made their mouths water. Rolls were put in to heat to crispness, onions were sliced, the cover was removed from a bowl of small cherry tomatoes and there was butter, lettuce, pickles, the usual condiments . . . and chili peppers. That last one made Bridget smile and shake her head.

There was a flat lazy-daisy cake with a broiled icing of butter, brown sugar and coconut. They ate, talked and teased. Bridget noted that while Jeremy looked at Bernice, his eyes stayed on her face, but when he looked at her, his eyes glanced down her body. Although she blushed, it pleased her that she attracted him.

Jeremy asked Bridget if she snow skied, and she said a little. Had he ever? He replied that he had. Had she ever sand skied? He knew about the Indiana dunes. She said no, had he? Yes, he had. Where? In Morocco. Morocco? What had he been doing there? He'd been sent over by the Department of Agriculture. Really? Why? Oh, he knew a thing or two about sheep.

The talk went on to adventure, like scuba diving off the Florida Keys and retrieving seventeenth-century ballast rocks. "I'll show you some when you see the arrowheads." And he spoke of flying over the western desert and, in all that vastness, suddenly seeing the pueblos tucked away under the cliffs. "That is a sight!"

Bernice's eyes were quiet as she listened.

Once Jeremy began a story, "After we won The War Between the States—"

Bridget protested, "We won! And it was the Civil War!"

"Now honey, how can you be so misinformed?" he questioned in mock concern.

"Misinformed! What about the history books?"

"They just don't make no never-mind, honeychild. History books can say anything. It just all depends on who pays the printer."

She laughed and bowed her head to acknowledge his point.

After their picnic, they cleaned up. That done, the blanket was too tempting, and they lay like four turtles, to talk sleepily and doze in the warm sun. Bridget said her mother's last letter mentioned the first dusting of snow in Indiana, and there she was...lazing in the hot TEXAS sun.

They called her a snow bird again. They told of the acres of parking areas all over the Citrus Valley where thousands of "Winter TEXANS" parked their trailers. They said how the Yankees invaded the orange and grapefruit groves to pick the fruit, causing dreadful damage to the trees with their carelessness. A little like the pecan poachers.

Bridget chided, "Surely the Yankees wouldn't take fruit the way they were threshing the trees for pecans?

If they only took a couple of oranges that wouldn't be so terrible."

"That's the way each of them thinks. It isn't a 'couple' of oranges. It's thousands. They do a great deal of damage to the crops. It's a problem." Little John explained.

"It seems exaggerated." Bridget wasn't really convinced.

"On top of that, the crops are already sold on the trees. Even if the owners of the groves wanted to, the fruit is no longer theirs to give away or to sell."

"I see."

"It would no doubt irritate an Indiana farmer if people invaded his fields of corn, and walked through, breaking down stalks to carry off 'only a couple of ears'?"

That put a new slant on the problem.

Their talk turned to where they'd like to go in the world. Bernice said New York, Bridget said Scotland, but neither man could see any reason for leaving TEXAS.

Jeremy rolled on his side, so that his back was to Bernice, and he possessively laid his arm across Bridget's waist. She turned her head and looked at him. His eyes watched her from under the shadow of his Stetson. Their exchange was very serious as they contemplated each other. He winked slowly. It was like a caress.

She listened to him breathe and saw the pulse in his throat. He was alive. So male. He was a strong individual. A person. She had no intention of capturing

his heart. She wanted only a brief affair, before she left
TEXAS.

Sighing, she turned her head away to look through
the branches at the clear sky. It was lovely in TEXAS,
but it wasn't home. She was honest enough to realize
that Jeremy was attracted to her. He could care for
her. He was so careful of her, that she could hurt him
with her carelessness.

He'd talked about them seeing each other on a long-
term basis. Once he'd mentioned grandchildren. Why
couldn't he be casual about this fling? Why couldn't
he just relax, let her flirt with him, seduce him and
simply be her TEXAS experience?

He was very sweet, funny and nice. She remembered the kids at school and how they liked him.
Everyone liked him. How could she risk hurting him?
She couldn't so she would cool it. She would be a visitor with good manners and no involvement.

"What's going on in that busy little mind of
yours?"

His breath stirred the hair by her ear in an intimate
caress and her senses reacted quite amazingly. But it
was time to begin. "Your arm weighs a ton. My ribs
are sagging."

He cupped his hand around her ribs and pulled her
close to him. "That'll brace them."

"You rebels are very clever."

"It wasn't us that invented Yankee dimes. I think all
you Yankees have only one thing on your minds. You
just come down here to sow your wild oats and break
our hearts." She looked so startled that he was bemused. He wondered why she should look surprised.

She lifted his arm off her stomach and rose to her feet in a nicely fluid movement. Her good muscles had begun in her cheerleading days. He followed her up as effortlessly. He was an awesomely powerful man. It was going to take all her self-discipline to keep her hands off him.

Little John also stood, and he reached down to pull Bernice to her feet. Then he picked her up and carried her around, walking with ease. She lay in his arms, with her head on his shoulder and allowed him to do that. Little John looked down and smiled at Bernice then his arms lifted her to him as he bent his head and kissed her. She didn't object.

Jeremy whispered to Bridget, "I think Bernice is getting over me."

Bridget watched too, thinking how simple Bernice's life was, compared with her own.

The Peterses came by at ten-thirty on Sunday morning to take the Taylors to the eleven o'clock worship service. The church sat alone in the midst of nowhere, with its tombstones like a mushroom garden on one side and the parsonage on the other. Mark was very attentive and shared a hymnal with Bridget who, with her ruined vocal chords, hadn't been allowed to sing, even in a group, since high school days.

Jeremy was there, looking gorgeous in a suit and tie. Bridget pensively watched the back of his head all through the service and didn't hear a word. He came to say hello afterward, giving her a conspiratorial wink. What could the conspiracy be? she pondered as she drove with her dad and the Peterses to The Club, an unimaginative rectangular building sitting by an eight-hole golf course.

Puzzled, Lawrence inquired, "Eight holes?" Whoever heard of an eight-hole golf course?

"That's all the money and room we had at the time," Mark explained. "Whoever wins the eighth hole gets to choose which of the eight to replay to make the required nine holes." Then Mark asked if Bridget played golf. She said no, though Lawrence volunteered that he did. Mark didn't hear that because he was telling Bridget that he was just the man to teach her how to play, and from his look and his pronunciation of "play," he wasn't talking about golf.

Inside The Club were round, bare, scrubbed tables, wooden chairs and a bare scrubbed plank floor. The windows were sparkling clean. Just as they were ordering, Jeremy came in escorting a very attractive woman who had to be thirty-five if she was a day. Jeremy acted very surprised to see them and came over to ask if he and his aunt could join them? Mark said, "Of course," and rose to his feet, to freeze there, staring at Jeremy's aunt. As she came to the table, he questioned, "Matilda?" and his voice sounded strange: young, uncertain.

She smiled, with easy graciousness and said, "Well, hullo, Mark," as she gave him her hand.

"Matilda!" he exclaimed, unaware that anyone else was around. It was obvious that he was stunned as he held her hand in both of his and continued to stare.

Jeremy grinned fatuously at Bridget and busily edged two chairs between Mark's and Bridget's as he introduced Matilda to Bridget and Lawrence. They smiled their greetings as they shifted chairs to accommodate the new arrivals.

Matilda's blue eyes sparkled electrically as she acknowledged them. Mark continued to hold her hand, with his eyes glued to her lovely face. Jeremy seated his aunt and sat down by Bridget. Matilda looked up at Mark. He finally released her hand, and he sat down slowly. "Matilda," he said, very intensely, unbelievingly, but for the third time.

She wasn't the least boggled. Very confident and assured, she was tall and elegant with a cap of shiny ash-blond curls and a sweet mouth. She said to Mark, helping his limited conversational scope seem normal. "It's nice to see you again, Mark."

"Yes," he replied, for whatever that meant.

They had baked ham, yams, green beans, applesauce and small corn muffins for dinner, with peppermint ice cream for dessert. Mark did eat, but he didn't pay any attention to his food...only to Matilda.

Bridget had already figured out that Jeremy's Aunt Matilda was his secret weapon, but Mark's stunned reaction at seeing her made Bridget know there was more to it all than Just Old Friends. It made her pensive. Everyone was pairing up but her. She had to back away from a willing man and leave him alone.

Mark finally pulled himself together and, unknowingly disrupting the table conversation, asked bluntly, "I thought you were working abroad?"

"I was. With NATO." She smiled at him. "But after the first of the year, I asked to be transferred back to the States. I'm based in DC now, but I'd particularly like to be back in TEXAS. I long to be home again."

"You do?" he asked with riveted interest.

"Yes. I miss my friends." Then she turned to Bernice and commented, "May I say what a lovely young woman you've become?"

Bernice showed she was taking yet another step over into adulthood by replying simply, "Thank you," as they measured one another with friendly interest. Bernice knew Matilda and had heard something of her story.

Jeremy ate with gusto, his lips quirked now and again and his crinkles deepened, as he slid smug glances at Bridget. Gloomily, Bridget thought he'd fixed things for Mark and Matilda. Why couldn't he fix things for her? And she heard Bernice ask Jeremy if he'd seen Little John? See? Jeremy had fixed that, too.

Jeremy replied to Bernice, "He pulled duty today. They're looking for something." Bernice frowned at his words as though she worried about Little John.

Mark was asking Matilda how long she would be home? And she replied that she had to return to DC the next day. "So short a time?" His deep voice was serious.

"This time." Her reply held promise.

"Do you have plans until you leave?" He really was pushy, Bridget thought, but Matilda didn't seem to mind at all.

"None."

"Oh, Auntie," J.R. interrupted wickedly. "I thought I'd take you over to the home place and show you what I've..."

Matilda's eyes danced in recognition of his sassiness. "Not this time."

"I'd like to be with you." Mark hadn't actually heard J.R.

"All right." She gave him her smile.

Lawrence observed their manner with one another, and his regard was envious. He missed his wife, Jean, so badly... just to talk to her, to look at her, to touch her.

After their meal, Matilda drove off with Mark and Bernice, leaving J.R. to drive the Taylors home. Bridget said, "There goes my career as a femme fatale."

"Feeling dumped?" J.R. gave mock sympathy.

"Right now I think Mark would have trouble remembering my name!"

Lawrence tousled her hair and agreed. But Jeremy put a casual arm across Bridget's shoulders and told her, "Don't worry, honey, I still love you." He looked into her father's eyes and smiled. Then, as he drove them home, J.R. told them he'd called his aunt the night before, and she'd just flown in that morning from DC. He said Mark had been twenty-four years old when he first came to this Promised Land. Matilda had been fifteen and had fallen totally in love with him. Mark had been attracted, but he'd thought Matilda far too young.

Then Bernice's future mother came on a visit to the area. She had been a couple of years older than Mark and had simply dazzled him. They had eloped in a shockingly short time, and Matilda had cried for a week. She'd never married. After she was graduated from college, she didn't return home. To see a married Mark was just too painful to think about, and she had left the country entirely.

When Mark's wife died last winter, Matilda had flown home, but he'd been away traveling. It seemed when Jeremy's aunt was in TEXAS, Mark wasn't. So that day was the first time they'd seen each other in years. J.R. knew Matilda still cared for Mark, and seeing Mark's reaction, it sure looked as though he wasn't totally indifferent to her.

As Jeremy drove the Taylors into their lane, he said his own parents were due back just anytime. They'd gone down to Australia, where it was spring, to visit friends who also raised sheep. The two men had met during the Korean War. They had continued their friendship, sharing information on sheep and visiting now and then.

At the Taylors' house, Cassius was glad to see Jeremy. The big man squatted down to rub the dog's head and body. Bridget watched as Cassius had to close his eyes to hold in the happiness. It seemed everyone loved Jeremy. She could too but she had to be careful she did not. She not only had to protect Jeremy from hurt, but herself as well.

The Taylors had put a thick soup in the slow cooker that morning, and the stingy cooker allowed only the very faintest mouth-watering whiff to escape to tantalize them. J.R. drew a deep, appreciating breath and smiled, so Lawrence invited him for supper. The invitation sobered Bridget, for it meant that Jeremy would be there all day, and she would see him every time she glanced up.

It was a fine afternoon. As Bridget worked needlepoint on a canvas to cover a brick doorstop, her father and J.R. sat at the wicker table on the porch and played chess.

Later, while Lawrence typed notes in his room, J.R. and Bridget strolled to the river with Cassius. When they returned to the house, it was to find that the Miner cousins from San Antonio were there. They'd brought the Taylors two loaves of homemade bread. It was easy to convince them to stay for supper, too, since there was plenty of rich, delicious soup. Unfortunately they also ate all the gift bread—in thick slices with lots of butter.

After they cleared away the dishes and put the food away, they strolled down to inspect the pig. "You've named him? You're kidding! How can you eat a pig you've *named*?"

The pig continued his aloof and rude behavior. Before dark they all played pitch and catch, and the cousins became acquainted with Jeremy. They all ganged up on the Taylors, teasing them about being Yankees. Sara didn't help. She said she was a TEXAN by osmosis, and if they stayed long enough, they too would be able to pass.

The cousins drove back to the city, but Jeremy lingered to see if the moon really came up in that part of the county, too. It had been a lazy pleasant day. Bridget knew Jeremy was going to kiss her. She decided she would permit him one more before she quit kissing

him altogether. But Jeremy's good-night kisses ruined
Bridget as a functional being, and probably scorched
the grasses and the nearby trees. He had Bridget
gasping, clenching her hands in his shirt and making
hair-raising little sounds in her throat that about
turned him inside out.

Bridget had a tough time prying herself out of bed
on Monday morning because she'd slept very poorly.
She and Cassius walked to the store to inspect the
completely rigged snow fencing. Mrs. Smith was very
pleased with the lessened glare. The change was
marked.

"See Cassius is still with you."

"Yep." She made an effort to be cheerful. "Notice
that 'yep'? I'm getting acclimatized." They shared a
grin, then Bridget said, "Did you know Jeremy's Aunt
Matilda was in town yesterday—just for the day?" She
threw in that little ringer.

"She *was*?" The old lady was electrically interested.

Mrs. Smith wasn't unlike a lot of Bridget's relatives. "Umm-hmm. And Mark took her to his house
for the afternoon, and to the airport this morning."

"Hooray and hallelujah! That's been a long time
getting righted. That Matilda is a special girl." Though
her words were jubilant, her face was serious and kind.

"Mrs. Smith, you're a fine woman."

"You're not too bad yourself...for a Yankee." She
slid that in with a slight smile. "I think maybe you
ought to think about settling down here."

"It's too far from home. I'd miss my family. My kin. I feel I'm an outsider here, and it's too dangerous down here with all the warnings about opening windows, watching out for snakes and staying out of dry river beds, although even in Indiana we have to worry about rustlers."

"It's no more dangerous than anywhere else. Everywhere in the world there are things wrong, or bad, that are peculiar to that place. I know you warn people up north to stay in their cars when they're caught driving in a blizzard. To open windows in a house in case of tornados, in order to reduce air pressure changes. To stay off thin ice . . . and never to run a car engine with the windows all closed. It's just important to know what to watch out *for*, what the danger *is*, and it makes life interesting. Without some danger, life would be dull."

"I didn't think of it that way. You're right."

"I've always been right, honey, except for that one time when I thought I was wrong but I was right." They laughed together. "How are the plants doing?"

"Just fine. They look so strong and pretty on the porch."

"You watering them right?"

Some people can't let go of things, so Bridget assured Mrs. Smith, "Perfectly."

"Take care of them now, you hear?"

That afternoon the sun was too friendly, the air was still and it was hot. Bridget donned her bathing suit and went down to the river. There she found a sun-warmed pool that had a rope hanging from a tree limb

extending out over the water. The river bank was bare
and hard, beaten down by many feet. Up on the bank,
a four-by-four chunk of wood was imbedded in the
dried mud for a step. Obviously that was the take-off
point for a swing on the rope.

Bridget walked around with Cassius to be sure there
wasn't a soul anywhere around. The only sounds she
heard were the cypress trees sieving the breeze and the
birds discussing their own business. Having been
trained never to take anything for granted, especially
the depth of water, Bridget gingerly tested the water's
depth before cautiously trying a rather timid swing on
the rope. It was exhilarating! With all the trees, Cassius on guard and the complete silence, she felt that
she, Cassius and the birds were the only living things
around. With the dog there, there couldn't even be any
snakes.

She stripped off her wet swimsuit and hung it over
a branch. She climbed gleefully to the step and swung
out over the water, to drop with a loud splash. It was
glorious. She climbed and swung and splashed and
swam and paddled and floated . . . and loved it.

In such a silence, the sound of a splash carries a long
way.

Tuesday she made a repeat swim, just as nice, just
as refreshing, just as private. Cassius watched her,
entertained, but he couldn't be coaxed into the water.

Wednesday she substituted for the sixth grade.
They, too, called her "Miss Taylor, honey" in friendly
impudence. But she was firm that "Miss Taylor" was
sufficient. One sassy boy, who was taller than she,
suggested just "honey," but she quelled him with such

an icy look that she made him chuckle in his young male throat.

On Thursday, after having to skip a day, Bridget eagerly arrived at her pool about two-thirty. She listened carefully, stripped naked, climbed to the four-by-four, swung out and splashed joyfully into the water. She surfaced, flipped back her hair with a satisfied grin—and looked straight into Jeremy's amused, intensely interested eyes as he squatted on the riverbank, petting Cassius.

"What are you doing here!" She was so shocked that she blushed scarlet and sank down until the water was up to her mouth.

"I needn't ask you that! My, you are a *sight* swinging on that rope, Jane." He rose and began to unbutton his shirt.

"What are you doing?" She gasped and went pale, moving so she could stand on the silt-covered icy river bottom.

"Me Tarzan. Me swim."

"No!"

"Now, honey, that's just plain selfish!"

"Go a-way!" She was simply furious. "Cassius, you *are* a traitor. I should have known!"

Jeremy smiled down at Cassius, then stopped still. "Hush!" he said sharply, listening rather elaborately. She listened with breathless alarm, but heard nothing. Jeremy exclaimed furiously, "I knew they'd be here!" He whistled a shrill blast, waved his arms and yelled, "Get back to work!" There was a crash through the brush as bodies fled.

Bridget gasped in horror and choked on an almost swallowed gulp of river water. She coughed as Jeremy invited her: "Come on out. They've gone now. Come here and I'll pat your... back for you." He smiled.

"They were *watching*!" she sputtered in embarrassment.

He settled his holster, knuckled back his Stetson, leaned against the convenient cypress which had its roots in the water and began to roll a cigarette. "You're too enticing a picture with your nude afternoon swim, and the work's being neglected."

He was very clever. He didn't actually say there *were* "watchers" because truthfully no one else was really there. J.R. had investigated Monday's splashing and it was he who wasn't getting his work done. So he'd stationed two of his superbly trained sheepdogs—each with an unbelled ewe—who were admonished to be absolutely still until he signaled. Remarkably the stupid sheep did stand silently, eating the fresh silage J.R. had placed for them. At J.R.'s signal whistle, the dogs herded their charges, crashing through the underbrush, back to the pasture. It was well done and J.R. was very pleased with himself.

Appalled, Bridget continued to choke and cough but she managed, "Jeremy! Go away! I mean it! I'm getting cold!"

All was peaceful. Gus moved into view behind J.R. and Cassius loped back to greet the horse who shook his head rattling his reins. Jeremy glanced up lazily to grin at Bridget. Suddenly he blanched, and dropped the unlit cigarette as he whipped his gun out and fired, yelling *"Snake!"*

Bridget screamed and flinched. She rose from the water and stared at J.R. with a look of horror on her face. She stumbled up to the river bank. Her legs were like wet noodles, and her wet hair streamed down above her luscious naked body. She gasped, "It bit me..." and crumpled in a faint at his feet before he could catch her.

Chapter Seven

Having worked all his life with men and animals and away from town, Jeremy was no stranger to wounds of various kinds. He was skilled in first aid, and he could see that the bullet's crease had done very little damage.

Jeremy ripped off his shirt and gently eased Bridget into it. Then he took out his handkerchief and pressed it to her shoulder before he tied it there, tightly in place, with the bandanna from his throat. She finally came to and saw him bending close, peering intently into her eyes. She moaned faintly. "Oh, Jeremy..." and a big tear slid down her cheek.

"You're all right, honey." His voice was soft and earnest. "I killed the snake."

"Oh...." Another tear began its journey.

"*Honest*, honey, you *are* all right. The snake didn't bite you."

"Didn't...?" she questioned as she looked up at him with confused, sad, tear-blurred eyes.

He thought her teary eyes really did look like dew-drenched violets. He comforted her, "No, it didn't bite you. I shot you."

She frowned a little. "You what?"

"I shot you," he explained matter-of-factly. "The snake was too close so I had to nick you in order to kill it."

She struggled up. "You shot me?" she asked, not believing it. Her voice squeaked up.

"Honey, better shot than bit any day. Water moccasins are nasty things. And anyway, it's just a little old nick. No sweat."

"You *shot* me?" She was beginning to get indignant.

"Simmer down now, it's all right. Let's get your trousers on and—"

She jerked her head down to look at her body and saw his shirt covering her, the long tails down almost to her knees. There was only one way it could have been put on her, and she blushed crimson.

"We'll go over to my place and fix it. Then after we check it out with Doc, I'll drive you on home."

She sat up, and J.R. brought her clothes over and whistled as he commented on her flamboyant underwear, knowing it'd make her angry. Being mad would give her enough adrenaline in her system to get her to the house.

Bridget put her hands to her face and moaned, "I'll just die." She meant of embarrassment.

He helped her to stand up. "No you won't, honey. I'm going to save your life and then you'll belong to me just like all us Chinese say."

"You're not Chinese."

"I've read Confucius and that practically makes me a native—put on your underwear—and he says plain as day, 'If Jeremy Robert Winsome saves Bridget...' What's your middle name, honey?"

She snatched her panties, turned her back and stepped into them under the screening tail of his shirt. Jeremy frowned at her blood staining the shoulder of his shirt. "What's your middle name, honey? His voice had turned gentle.

"Willis," she replied shortly.

"Will-is?" He was unbelieving in order to goad her. "Yes!"

"Willis." He tasted it. "I like it. It says—now pay attention, Willis, honey—"

"Jeremy..." she warned.

Quite firmly, he went on, "It says: 'If Jeremy Robert Winsome saves Bridget Willis Taylor's life, then she *belongs* to him.' See? And you just can't hardly quarrel with old Confucius. Here, put your trousers on. I'll help."

"Get away from me!" She was having trouble pulling the trousers up her legs, which were still damp from her swim. He watched the blood stain spread farther on her shoulder and simply reached out and pulled her trousers up. She jerked away and buttoned the band then zipped them up with hands trembling from shock.

He wadded her own shirt and lay it on that shoulder and told her to hold her hand on it. He whistled for Gus to come close. "I'll help you get on."

Through her teeth she said, "I'm not riding that beast."

"Gus, did you hear that? She called you a beast!" Jeremy exaggerated his offense. He knew her shock wasn't entirely from the wound. The snake, the supposed "watchers" and emerging naked from the river had all contributed to her dismay.

"Why does he always hang his head down that way?" Bridget was suspicious of the horse and backed away from him until she pushed against Jeremy's hard tanned naked chest.

He steadied her and held her against him. "We were riding hell-bent one day and he stepped into a hole and fell hard! He's never really trusted me since..."

"Him...too?"

"And he goes along watching for his own gopher holes. He raises his head only when he's racing, or if he sees a tasty filly."

Gus raised his head and looked at Bridget, having smelled her blood. And J.R. scolded, "No, Gus, she's a human female." He grinned down at Bridget.

"I'm not going to ride on that animal. Which way do I walk?"

"You are...*the*...most contrary female I have ever had to deal with! *Get on that horse!*"

She protested, "He just isn't a proper horse. With his head hanging down that way, I'd feel as if I was on top of a...hay stack!'' Due to her slight case of shock, she was amused by the ''hay stack'' analogy.

"Hay burner," Jeremy corrected. "Get on! I'll hold you, and then you'll feel secure, and Gus will walk with his head up. You hear me, horse? Cassius, you go on ahead and scout for pot holes for Gus." And the dog did—or at least, he did go on ahead.

J.R. put Bridget's foot in the stirrup and boosted her bodily as she protested, "Feel secure with you? How could I possibly feel secure with a man who deliberately shot me?"

J.R. ignored her. He took her foot out of the stirrup and hoisted himself up to ride behind her, his forearms supporting her as she wobbled a bit. Then he eased her back against him, and they began the ride to his place. It wasn't far. It only seemed so.

"My shoulder hurts."

"I know," he said gently. "But it's not at all bad." He knew it hurt. "We'll be there in just a minute, and I'll make you more comfortable, before I take you to Doctor Fell."

"A doctor? Why do I..."

"Have to... They're just real ugly about us shooting one another. Now, if someone gets shot, we have to tattle. I don't know how it is in Indiana, but in TEXAS we have to report gunshot wounds. Since any wound needs looking after, we'll report to Dr. Fell. And for God's sake, Willis honey, try to refrain from mentioning that poem to Dr. Fell."

"What poem?"

"You know, 'I do not like thee, Doctor Fell...' He's sick of it."

"A sick doctor," she commented musingly, and shook her head.

They rode silently, and Jeremy watched her. "I noticed you're an inny, although I do admit I didn't notice *right* away."

"Any? Any what?" she asked, confused.

"Your leedaloo. You're an inny."

"Leedaloo?" More confused.

"Your tummy button...navel."

"Oh?" Still confused.

"Yours goes in." He hugged her. "So does mine." He kissed her cheek. "We match...there." He chuckled as she blushed.

She questioned, "Leedaloo?"

"Yeah. Probably a Swiss word." He yodeled, "Oh, le-e-da-loo, Oh, le-e-da-loo." And he was rewarded by her grin. "You do know why we have them, don't you?"

"That's where God pokes us to see if we're done?"

"No. That's for the salt when we eat celery in bed."

She groaned. "That joke was in Noah's library."

"See? It's stood the test of time."

As they neared the yard of his place, Bridget asked carefully, "Uh...we'll be alone, won't we?"

"Yeah.

She persisted: "No one else will...be there?"

"No." His interest was completely captured.

"Are you sure?"

"We'll be all by our little selves, Willis honey." He hugged her.

She relaxed back against him and sighed. "Good."

Her reply made him look down quickly at her, and he saw a faint smile. He misunderstood her, as he felt the stronger stirrings of desire, and he allowed the reins of his control to loosen. Jeremy slid off Gus and reached to lift her down.

She was hesitant and looked around as she repeated, "Are you sure no one else is here?"

He set her on the ground. "No one anywhere around at all."

He hugged her to his hairy bare chest and gave her a brief kiss. "You are so sweet." She stiffened, and he laughed in great anticipation. "I know, I know, you want to get cleaned up first."

"Please." She felt yucky and didn't want to see the doctor until she had cleaned up.

His voice was low and his eyes adoring. "But I can hardly wait."

"Do I look that ghastly?" She pushed back her river-wet hair that was drying in lanks.

"You're gorgeous." And he meant it.

The opened wide, V-shaped house was old. The siding of silvered boards that hadn't been painted in years. The long narrow floor-to-ceiling windowpanes of the rooms glinted in their old, wavering imperfections. All the rooms had tall doors opening onto the porch, which was only a step from the ground. There was a railing between every other pair of the wooden porch pillars, and chairs were placed by them so that, in the evening after-supper rest, you could lean back and put your feet up on a rail.

Gus walked with them, in under the low sheltering limbs of the great live oak, and J.R. dropped Gus's reins across the porch rail as he told the horse, "Behave yourself, hear?" They crossed the porch in the middle of the V and entered there. A bath had been added next to the kitchen just in the last few years. In it, there was no light and no mirror. He unbuttoned his shirt that was on her and slipped it from her. She picked up a towel and covered her breasts.

He laughed low in his throat, with tender indulgence, and he teased her lovingly, "So modest? I've already seen that you're different from me. I don't mind."

He had dropped the bloody shirt on the floor behind her, and standing in front of her, he carefully undid his bandanna from her shoulder and threw it and his blood-soaked handkerchief on top of the bloody shirt. Then he gently cleaned the drying blood from her shoulder and back with a clean, wet, warm cloth. He peered at the wound and said, "It's fine. Just a crease. It's setting nicely." As he finished with the bandage, he felt he should ask, "You're sure you want to do it now, Willis honey?" His question was meltingly tender.

"Absolutely." She was positive. She thought he meant to get clean. "Can I take a shower?"

"How about later?" His voice was deep and soft as he leaned to kiss her. "Let's go in there." He turned her toward the hall.

She started to protest, but she looked down and saw the bloody cloths and shirt. It looked ghastly! "Is that *my* blood? That's *my* blood!" she answered herself, and she fainted again.

Her first semiconscious thought was how marvelously comfortable she was. Then slowly she was dreamily aware that her body was experiencing delicious sensations. She felt her hand at the back of Jeremy's head, and it seemed to her that he was kissing her in a very thrilling way, and then she began to kiss him back with great pleasure. "Jeremy?" she questioned.

"Oh, Willis honey." His whisper was husky as his mouth returned to hers, kissed her deeply, his tongue flicking in a caress along her opening lips and touching hers.

"Jeremy!" She was shocked, and she pushed against him.

He protested, "Hey, honey..."

She had to stop him. Not just for his sake, but for hers. This could be addictive, and she was going home to Indiana. "Jeremy!"

Puzzled, he raised his head and looked at her. "Now why are you being so unfriendly?" Her eyes were enormous and strangely troubled.

What could she tell him? All he was doing was kissing her. "You were kissing me."

"Well, of course."

"Why are you doing this?"

"Well...I started out giving you mouth-to-mouth resuscitation? But you distracted me." He sighed dramatically. "It's been a long, un-nerving day." He grinned with great charm and settled back down, to bury his face against the side of her throat, nibbling there, his whiskery face hot and damp with sweat.

Again Bridget pushed at him. "What do you think you're doing?"

"I'd think that was fairly obvious."

"How dare you!"

"What do you mean 'How dare...' I? Honey, what are you trying to do to me? Look, you gave me all those signs. And there surely could be no question in your mind that I am more than willing?"

"What signs?" She frowned, trying to remember if she'd done or said anything that he could have mis-understood.

"You kept asking if we'd be alone and..."

"Alone! I wanted to know if I'd have to face any of the men who'd been watching me swim."

Jeremy, knowing there had been no "men" watching at the river—only sheep and dogs—hadn't even considered that. It began to dawn on him that he had misunderstood, but he resisted that knowledge. "Oh, God, Willis, you've just got to be sweet to me now. You can't abandon me like this."

While they argued, her hand lay on the back of his head, toying with his hair in a soothing way that was very nice...for her. "We must stop." She sighed, and he was thrilled to his toenails to hear the regret in the sigh, but she added, "I have to get up."

"Willis?"

"No. But I'm sorry."

"You have no idea what you've done to me."

"I can't help it."

He pulled away and looked at her for an intense, desperate second. "You're lucky," he said as he got up and walked away.

Her body was filled with strange longings, but she noticed too that her legs were weak and her shoulder hurt. She sat up on the bed, aware the shower still ran. When she finally heard it turned off, she gingerly got off the bed.

Jeremy came into the room wearing only jeans. His hair was still wet from his shower. He looked at Bridget, standing there, her heart in her big eyes. He'd started to go to the huge old walnut chest, but drawn by her, he went to her. "It's okay, honey. I'll live, but only just." He tilted her face up to his and kissed her lightly. His hands and face were still cold from his long shower. "I'm sorry, too, that I misunderstood you; and I'm letting you get away—this time. Do you still want that shower?"

"No, thank you, but could I have a clean shirt?"

"Sure." His voice was gentle. He opened one of the chest drawers and pulled out the shirts, giving one to her as he undid the other for himself.

She turned her back to him, undid the buttons and began to ease her arm into the sleeve.

Jeremy came up in back of her and helped her into the shirt. "I love you, Willis honey. Today should show you how much." He turned her body just enough so that he could kiss her. He could have convinced her then to get back into bed, but he released her and walked toward the door saying, "I'll get the pickup." He stopped in the doorway, put his fist on the doorjamb and leaned his head against it.

"Are you all right?" She went to him and lay an anxious hand on his arm.

He straightened. "You've got me standing on my ear."

"Oh, Jeremy." Why didn't he know how tough it was for her too? Did he think he was the only one with a problem?

He sighed. "When you think of the thousands of times we'll make love in our lives, one more shouldn't matter."

"We haven't talked of marriage."

"That's what this whole conversation has been about."

When they reached the front door, Bridget hesitated cautiously, peeking out. "Can you see anyone, you know, who was down by the river?"

He assured her, "I guarantee all the peekers are out in the back pasture."

"Thank goodness."

Jeremy unsaddled Gus and put him into the barnyard. Cassius got into the pickup with them, and they drove slowly down the two-track lane. Bridget was about to get out to open and then wait to close the gate, but Jeremy made her sit still while he did it, and wouldn't allow her to use her shoulder to drive the truck through the gate.

As he reentered the pickup, she smiled blindingly at him. His answering smile was a trifle rueful. She *would* smile at him that way when she was comparatively safe. He thought she looked unutterably seductive in his shirt with her tangled hair, those blue eyes, and her sweet sweet smile. Her mouth...his body's senses were filled with her. They drove on in silence. Jeremy stopped at the stop sign when they came to the

paved road. He leaned his head on the steering wheel
as he groaned.

She asked, "Jeremy? What's the matter?"

"I feel like I was rode hard and put away wet, and I
wish..."

Not being familiar with that expression Bridget
didn't reply at first. Then she said that he could take
her home, if he liked, that her shoulder felt all right,
and she really didn't need a doctor.

He straightened up, and after checking the highway, he turned onto it as he said, "After all the trouble I've gone through today, I can't have you dying of
lead poisoning."

"*Lead* poisoning?"

"When someone's shot, we say, 'He died of lead
poisoning.'" He watched her frown. "You do know
bullets are made of lead?"

"You have an interesting view of things down here."

"I sure had an interesting view for a little while back
there." He slanted a glance to see her blush. "You'd
make a terrible nurse, fainting at the sight of blood
like that."

"I only faint when it's my blood. Anyone else's
doesn't bother me at all."

"Are you hardhearted in other ways beside being
mean to me?"

"Other people's blood doesn't seem serious to me
because I'm sure, being a Taylor, that I can cope. My
own blood seems a grave problem."

He laughed and they drove away in silence.

"Jeremy, I wasn't being mean to you. But you surprised me. I mean, I came to and it was so nice, but

Mother always said, 'Never get in a position to be a victim.' And I woke up not only in a very compromising position, but . . . liking it. It shocked me.'' Her foggy voice squeaked.

"*Did* you like my loving, Willis honey?''

"Oh, Jeremy.'' Her softened tone made her voice squeak worse, and her eyes were so tender he almost ran off the road. Then she added the ringer, "But...''

"Are you going to make me wait until we're married?''

"Marry you? That would be impossible. We haven't known each other very long, and we'll be going home in the spring. You see—''

Quite exasperated, Jeremy exclaimed, "My God, woman, I told you I love you right in front of your daddy! What does it take to convince you? Shall I go down on my knees? You are such a *trial* to me!''

"You cannot be serious.''

"We'll talk about it,'' he said as they turned off the highway into the yard of the clinic. "It's a two-bed hospital, too. Just be glad you don't have to stay here. Those two mattresses are as narrow and hard as your cold heart, Willis honey.''

"When did you have to stay here?''

"I broke my shoulder when Gus stepped into that hole that time.'' He got out of the truck and helped her out. Cassius stayed where he was. "I'm just glad it was my shoulder and not Gus's. We would've had to shoot him, and that would have broken my heart.'' He opened the clinic door.

"See? You're not serious about me. You shot me and your heart's not broken.''

"I wouldn't know about my heart or its condition. You have it. But I'd surely hate to have to choose between you and Gus." Then he called, "Hey! Lissa?"

"J.R.!" The voice was lilting, delighted, and a darling little blonde came into the room, her cheeks dimpling at the sight of Jeremy. Then she saw Bridget and the smile was noticeably less welcoming. "Oh ... hello," she said in a rather flat voice.

"This is Melissa Allen? Lissa, have you met Bridget Taylor?"

"No," she replied. She didn't seem too eager to meet her either.

Bridget smiled at the nurse as Lissa eyed the man's shirt on Bridget.

J.R. asked, "Doc in?"

"Yes. What's the trouble?"

Off-handedly he replied, "I shot Bridget here in the shoulder."

"You did what?"

From another room Dr. Fell heard. "Come on in, J.R., and bring your victim."

He was already pulling an instrument tray up by the examining table. He was a tall alert man about eighty years old with a slight paunch, thick gray hair and bifocals. "She all right?"

"Oh, sure. I didn't mean it serious."

When the examination was over, Jeremy insisted on paying the fee. Bridget objected, but he explained, "I shot you. I pay. It's only fair."

"I'm not sure I appreciate the favor."

"You're just lucky I'm such a good shot."

She knew that was true, but she scoffed, "Good!" They said goodbye to the doctor and the nurse and went out to the pickup, still disagreeing on his marksmanship. J.R. was explaining how clever he'd been to ricochet the bullet off her shoulder...

They drove off, still arguing, with Cassius sitting on the back seat of the truck. Dr. Fell's nurse, Melissa, stood in the window and watched them drive away. She said crossly, "Nobody in my entire family has ever liked Yankees."

Dr. Fell chuckled.

Chapter Eight

On the way to the Taylor place, J.R. stopped at a beer hall for beer, hot ham-and-cheese sandwiches and huge dill pickles. When they arrived at the house, Cassius went off as Miss Pru greeted them cordially.

On the table was a note saying Lawrence had gone to Sam Hughes's and would be back around ten o'clock.

Bridget filled the kettle to heat water for a bath, while J.R. laid out the supper on the table. He noted the new place mats, made from the same material as the sofa pillows. Jeremy had no trouble eating his and Lawrence's share, although he did give Miss Pru some of the melted cheese. She was addicted to cheese. He fed Cassius outside.

When the teakettle whistled, Jeremy carried it into the bathroom, pouring its boiling contents into the tub. He added cold water to make the bathwater a comfortable temperature and offered silkily to scrub her back. She declined, telling him to go on home, that she could manage. And she thanked him for an—interesting—different day.

But when she came into the living room in her long cotton flannel nightgown, he was still there. As nice as the days were, the nights were chilly, and her pretty gown reached from her chin to her toes to her fingertips. She looked old-fashioned and utterly charming.

He'd just finished building a fire in the fireplace for Miss Pru, who had waited patiently beside him, watching his every move with interest. Bridget had rinsed her hair and wrapped it awkwardly in a towel. She smiled at J.R. as she crowded Miss Pru, so she could sit in front of the fire to dry her hair.

Jeremy brought one of the blue chairs from the table and sat in back of her. He moved her between his knees and began gently to towel her hair. When she got her brush, he took it and sat on the floor behind her to brush out the tangles. He told her he was good currying a horse too.

She'd taken the pill Dr. Fell had given to her and became relaxed, drowsy, and yawned and sighed. When her hair was dry and brushed into a silken brown curtain, he tugged her back against his chest and put his arms loosely around her. They sat there in the quiet, contented in the firelight with Miss Pru occasionally giving a brief purr of her approval.

Finally, Bridget was so sleepy that she had to go to bed. She kissed Jeremy sweetly, but briefly, without lingering. He said he'd just stick around and talk to her daddy when he got home. Then, having turned the radio on low, J.R. sat on the sofa and Miss Pru jumped up to join him there. He opened one of Lawrence's research books in order to distract himself from thinking of Bridget lying in bed not far from him. Anyway, it was only good sense to know something about Etruscans if that was one of Lawrence's interests.

To his surprise, he found the book fascinating. He was so interested that he put cigarette papers to mark several segments that he wanted to discuss. So complete was his concentration that when Lawrence arrived J.R. was surprised it was so late.

Lawrence exclaimed with pleasure, "Well, hello!" He looked around, "Where's Bridget?" But he was coughing so it was a little while until he could ask again, "Where's Bridget?"

"She's asleep. And, Mr. Taylor? She's just fine."

Something in J.R.'s tone caused Lawrence to look at him rather sharply, "Shouldn't she be?"

"Why don't you just step down the hall and take a peek at her so's you'll know."

"What's up?" Then intensely he questioned, "Did you two elope?"

"No," he responded to comfort her father, but he added curiously, "Would you have minded?"

"I don't believe so, but when she marries, we'd want to be there."

"And you wouldn't mind if I was the groom?"

"No," Lawrence said thoughtfully. "You seem like a good man. People are fond of you. Although your animals are disciplined they like you, so you must be gentle. You work hard and don't mind doing it. You seem a responsible citizen, being on the school board." Lawrence's glance sharpened. "Are you asking to marry her?"

"I am. But I don't think you should tell her that. She thinks she's so independent, and she keeps talking about going home, but there's something else. Have you any brandy?" When Lawrence shook his head, Jeremy asked, "Sherry?"

"Only beer. Damn it, J.R. what's going on? Spit it out!"

J.R. sighed. "She's just fine, really. But I shot her."

"You did *what*?" Lawrence wasn't quite so Taylor-calm and in control after all.

"That's funny. That's almost exactly what she said."

"She *said*?"

"Yeah. When I told her."

"You mean she didn't know it?"

"Well, she'd fainted and . . ."

"You shot her when she was unconscious?"

"Oh no. She'd fainted because of the snake."

"*The snake!* Jeremy, for God's sake, start from the beginning!"

So Jeremy told him all that had happened—except for a few minor details about the planted sheep, the fact that she'd been naked and that bedroom scene. He'd been saying "she" and "your daughter" and finally called her "Willis."

"Willis?"

J.R. was uncomfortable. "Well, 'Bridget' isn't one of my very most favorite names."

"Mine neither."

"Then how did you come to name her that?"

"Her mother, Jean, is a charmer. Bridget was our first child, and I was so mind-boggled by the miracle that I wasn't paying enough attention."

"Willis suits her. Dr. Fell..."

"Dr. Fell? 'I do not like thee, Dr....'"

"Don't you *ever* quote that to him."

"That bad, huh."

"Yep. But he says her shoulder is fine and should heal nicely. He's to peek at it Saturday morning. I'll come fetch her there. Okay?" At Lawrence's nod, Jeremy continued, "Uh...have you ever noticed your daughter tends to be just a mite contrary?"

"Takes after her mother's side. My side is calm, in control and pliant."

"Yeah. I've been noticing, and I heard what a *time* they had getting you to come on down here." He drawled it out.

Lawrence slanted Jeremy a look. "You've never seen her mother."

Jeremy nodded with understanding. "But I've seen the daughter." And they both nodded.

Lawrence did go look in on Bridget. Then he and J.R. settled down before the dying fire for a brief chat, but the talk turned to J.R.'s questions about the Etruscans, asking why, how and where. It was a satisfying conversation that lasted far past midnight, long after even Miss Pru had given up and gone down the hall to Bridget's room, and Jeremy's envious eyes had followed the cat.

* * *

Mrs. Smith came by the next morning, having heard about Bridget being shot. She came in a 1933 Model A Ford, which was in mint condition. She found Bridget sitting in the sun on the porch. It was a formal call and for a little while the old lady acted quite stiffly. She wore a hat and she brought Bridget a pot of beautiful deep-scarlet geraniums. She cast a very critical eye on the other plants and was somewhat astonished they still thrived. She needlessly tweaked off a leaf and fussed over them as if she had arrived just in time to save them from shriveling away.

She gave Bridget a penetrating eye and was satisfied that, like the plants, she'd live. "Heard J.R. shot you." Her voice was quite rough, but had a tell-tale quaver. Bridget realized the old lady had been alarmed about her, and she was very touched by Mrs. Smith's concern.

Lawrence joined them for tea, and Mrs. Smith admired the pillows and table mats. She was abrupt and awkward because she wasn't behind the store counter. She saw the picture of the bull. "Good. Yep. That's good," she commented and her eyes often drifted back to it thoughtfully.

She suggested that Bridget make some copies of it and do some drawings of the cactus. They'd put the drawings in her store to sell. And in the spring Bridget should paint the bluebonnets. There was always a good market for bluebonnet pictures because every TEXAS home was committed to have at least one such picture, it being the State Flower, and TEXANS being bone-deep patriots and all.

Bridget took Mrs. Smith through the tiny house, knowing she was curious, then down to admire the pig. Bridget confessed that she didn't much care for pigs, and Mrs. Smith said that, come spring, she could have a pig roast, which horrified Bridget. Mrs. Smith laughed at her.

Miss Pru had welcomed Mrs. Smith gracefully and the old lady smiled at the cat, then frowned. "No! Miss Pru I'm disappointed in you...again. In time for Christmas?" The cat just purred and blinked her eyes in a lazy, smug way.

With the dog and cat lazy in the sunshine, the Taylors cracked pecans and dug out the meats for holiday baking. Bridget thought Lawrence's cough wasn't quite so shattering and he looked better. A little tan surely did help anyone look healthier. She took an instant snapshot of him to send to her mother.

Bridget had already sent pictures of Jeremy, Little John, Bernice and one of Mrs. Smith sitting behind her counter at the store. And the school, the snow fencing, the house and of course, Cassius, Miss Pru and even the pig. That way the family would know who they would meet during the holiday. All the Taylors longed for the holidays.

Several days before the dance, Bridget had called Bernice from Mrs. Smith's store and asked what should she wear. Bernice told her to wear something comfortable because after the dancing started, the room became too warm. And although there would be a few women in trousers, why not wear a skirt for a dance? Bridget agreed.

So over a long lace-edged slip that she'd made, Bridget wore a dark red cotton dress which had a flounce around the bottom of the long full skirt. The top fitted her nicely shaped chest and waist. It had a scoop neck and short, almost puffed sleeves. With her dark hair loose, long loop earrings and the thin gold bangles on her wrists, only her blue eyes spoiled her gypsy look.

She had a white lace shawl her grandmother had crocheted from string. Its long fringe almost touched the floor. When she put that in the coat room at the dance, she heard an excited female voice saying, "J.R.'s here!" Another of the ninety-eight percent?

The dance was held in a big unattractive barn of a building on the fair grounds. Bridget saw it was a community dance, and whole families attended, so the place was noisy with giggles, laughter, a great deal of talk, even a shout or two. And there were fiddles and a bass added to the sound of a piano.

The littlest ones slept in baskets...and were admired and compared, tactfully, of course. Those children a little older danced and chased among the adults with squealing laughter and were hushed and told to behave, but not crossly. As the children finally fell asleep, chairs were pushed together, and the kids were covered with coats or jackets. When they could stay awake all evening, they considered themselves "older."

Some very old ladies sat on chairs placed around the edge of the dance floor. They discussed everybody else, who was kin to whom, and traits could be traced back through the years and pinpointed on some ancestor. Old scandals were referred to obliquely and relished with expressive brows, nodding heads and tucked-in mouths.

Just like in Indiana. Just like Taylors did. Just like home. But here, Bridget was the stranger, and she didn't know who people were, or the stories or gossip or their family histories. The touchstones were missing.

There were the inevitable separate groups of older men near the beer and women in the kitchen. Then there was the mixed group who danced. It included some of all ages, but was mostly made up of the in-betweens, the singles and the younger marrieds. All the groups were busy, noisy and sharing much laughter. It was a good time for just about everyone.

But there were the quarrels; some jealousy. Two people not speaking to each other were somewhere around. There were the peacemakers; the drunks. Just like Indiana. Just like home.

J.R. came to Bridget and led her to the dance floor. Close against his chest, she asked were any of the men there who'd watched her swim? He looked around, stretching, pretending to search, and said he couldn't see any of the "watchers" and he wouldn't worry if he were her.

"If I were *you*, I wouldn't! They wouldn't have watched you."

"And anyway, I doubt they'd recognize you—with your clothes on and all." He grinned at her, and she blushed. "Did I tell you that you look especially beautiful?"

Lawrence had been convinced to attend. He danced once, with Bridget, but mostly he stood around meeting some of the people and visiting. Bridget sat out the square dances.

The scoop neck of Bridget's gown was cut so that her bandage did show. J.R. accused her of wearing just such a dress to get all the sympathy she could, and she agreed. There were chiding comments, "J.R.! Has the Chamber of Commerce heard about this?" And "There *are* other ways to attract ladies' attention, you know." He grinned and let them tease him. He was a charming man.

Jeremy's grandparents were there. The Taylors were introduced to them, and the grandparents were welcoming and cordial. His grandmother was tall, slender and looked very like J.R. She was almost five inches taller than her husband. But he was burly and stockily formed, so that he was exceedingly masculine. His thick gray hair was somewhat unruly, and his eyebrows were thick, untamed and peaked.

While they stood talking, some of the first-graders approached shyly and squirmed as they said, "'Lo, Mith Taylor, honey. Hi, J.R." J.R. directed his full attention on them and returned their greeting.

"Are you going to marry Mith Taylor honey?" they asked giggling.

"Not . . . right away," J.R. replied.

Bridget gasped.

His grandparents laughed and several of the older men nearby joined the conversation, "Why not?"

Jeremy gave an exaggerated sigh of burden. "There's so much work to be done on her."

Bridget's squeaky, "Hah!" was ignored.

"Like—what?" the men teased, saying she looked pretty enough just the way she was. And the first-graders laughed, delighted to be a part of that adult conversation.

"Just for starters, she honestly thinks they won The War!"

"No!" they responded in chorus, as if they'd rehearsed.

"But . . ." Bridget tried.

"See?" He patiently explained to Bridget, "We did win. It's only our inbred courtesy that allows you all to think you won, since it seems so important to you Yankees. We know we won. The last battle was fought at Port Isabel down yonder on the TEXAS coast, and we won! The rest of the South had quit by then, but TEXAS hadn't."

She laughed with the rest and exclaimed, "Good grief! You never give up."

J.R. glinted a look. "That's right, honey. Not on anything."

His grandfather advised, "I wouldn't marry J.R. if I was you, honey."

Jeremy whispered in her ear, "He can call you honey because he's family."

His grandfather was going on, "Every woman within a hundred miles would be here, wanting to know how you caught him."

"He isn't going to marry me. I'm going home to Indiana in the spring."

"Are you sure?" He smiled a scowl at her. "We Winsome's never give up."

A man interposed, "Going to let Gus race that city slicker's horse at the fair, J.R.?"

"I've tried and tried to talk him out of it. I even had Mark Peters talk to him, but he seems bound and determined."

Sam Hughes left the dance early and dropped Lawrence off at the Taylor house. It wasn't long after that when Bridget suggested the Martins could drop her off. They had little kids who needed to be home in bed. Jeremy replied, "You came with me. I'll take you home." His voice lacked the usual soft teasing.

But he didn't take her home. He took her down one of the track roads that looked like all the others. He stopped the car, pushed the seat back and said, "Are you angry because I shot you?"

"Oh, no. That wasn't your fault."

"I did have to shoot you, Willis, in order to stop the snake from biting you. You have to know that. I'm not careless, nor did the bullet hit you because my aim was off. But it was necessary."

"Well. I understand."

"Why are you backing off from me? You said there's no one waiting for you, and you kiss like you're interested. What's the matter? Have I done anything to anger you or disgust you?"

"No, no, no! It's just that I could become very...involved with you. And I don't want to."

"Why not? I love you, Willis, honey. I want you to live here and become a genuine TEXAN. You can marry me and get a citizenship, and you can still be an Indianian."

"Oh, Jeremy. I don't want to live so far from home."

"This would be home; you'd be living right in the middle of it."

"So far from my family. Outside Sara and her family, I have no relatives at all down here."

"Honey, I have family enough for *five* wives, and they'll all be yours."

"You're prejudiced."

"How can you possibly accuse a TEXAN of being prejudiced?" His voice was soft. He'd put his arm along the back of the seat, and he'd moved over a little so he was quite close.

"You're teasing, while I'm trying to be serious."

"I'm deadly serious. You've got me scared. If it's only living in a strange place that's stopping you from loving me, this is a friendly land."

"It's so different down here. In February, you're already starting spring just as Indiana is getting its teeth into winter! I'm not sure I could adjust to being a TEXAN. It's too different. I'd always be a stranger."

"We all were in the beginning. You don't have to be here long to become a native. We're all parts of other nationalities. But now we're all TEXANS."

"You look like everyone else."

"No. Everyone else tries to look like us, but if you get up close, you can see the difference." He moved closer, then he kissed her. Again. And again. She murmured a feeble protest over his stroking and cuddling. He soothed her, "It's just appreciation, Willis honey. There's art appreciation, music appreciation and 'Willis' appreciation, but I sure as hell hadn't better catch anyone else appreciating you." He punctuated his argument with expert loving, kissing and as much appreciation as he could slip in. He drove her crazy.

The only reason Bridget wasn't seduced that night was that Jeremy wanted to be sure she knew what she was doing when he finally made love to her. He didn't want her to marry him from guilt or because she thought she had to. So he didn't actually make love with her. He sure curled her toes and muddled her brain and drove her body wild. Then to her great bewilderment, he took home the shambles that was left of her, removed her from his car, and put her inside the door of her house.

It was an excessively frustrated Bridget who went to her bed to toss and turn, as she faced the fact that she loved Jeremy. But could she love him enough to separate from her family? What was she to do? Could she live this far from home? A stranger in a strange land?

Then, just before the Thanksgiving Fair, J.R.'s parents returned from Australia, and Jeremy took Bridget and her father to meet them. A very nervous Bridget had developed a blinding headache and changed her dress three times. Lawrence laughed and said the Winsomes would realize how lucky they were to meet her.

Jeremy looked magnificent. He acted as if the day and the meeting were as ordinary as his suntan jeans. The Winsome house was big but not very impressive or ornate. It was made of adobe and surrounded by a grove of pecan trees and several great old oaks. The patio, in the center of the house, had a fountain. It was from the influence of the desert Moors' love of water, given to the Spanish, and brought to the New World.

Bridget was glad her father had such an easy manner, because it took her a while to settle down, relax and realize just how comfortable the Winsomes were to be around. They had J.R.'s blond looks. His dad's eyes were green and his mother's blue, the colors had melded in Jeremy's eyes. J.R. stayed beside her, held her hand and was amused because she was so nervous.

Matilda was there, with Mark close by her side. Mark greeted the Taylors in a friendly way, but his eyes were no longer interested in Bridget. Jeremy's sister and her husband had come from San Antonio to greet their parents' return. J.R.'s sister was especially dying to meet Bridget. The Winsome grandparents were also there, he burly and aggressive, and she like a slender taller reed that bent gracefully to the rock of him.

It seemed to Bridget everyone talked and all at once, but they were all very careful to be sure both Taylors were included in their conversations. Of course they teased J.R. terribly about shooting Bridget, and he replied he'd bagged his limit in women for the year.

And they teased the Taylors as they congratulated their intelligence for coming to TEXAS—always caps, did they know? And they inquired about Lawrence's progress on his book.

It was such easy company, that Bridget gradually relaxed, as her headache faded away. She watched how fond the Winsomes were with one another, and she was aware of their kindness to the Taylors. It especially pleased her that Jeremy felt so comfortable with his sister's children.

The Winsome parents knew so much about the Taylors that it was obvious J.R. must have been keeping in close touch with them by phone. They surprised Lawrence with an elegant wallet of kangaroo leather, and Bridget with a fine handbag of the same material. And they were shown opals of wondrous colors from Australia.

The talk became general. Bridget noticed the rug the grandmother was stitching in needlepoint and exclaimed over the scope of the undertaking. Their manner was so homey that it took a while before Bridget noticed the house. The furniture was plain, but antique and well cared for. The paintings excellent, the rugs luxurious, the garden flowers in odd lovely containers artfully placed, and the chairs and sofas elegantly comfortable. Although the house and its furnishings were subtle, it was all so posh that Bridget became thoughtful.

During dinner the conversation turned to the fair and the fact that Gus would race. Mr. Winsome chuckled. "No! You've found another victim?"

"And I can't convince him not to!" Jeremy shook his head in mock disgust, his eyes crinkling.

When they were leaving, the Winsomes admonished the Taylors: "Watch out for snakes on sunny days, never..."

"Never walk in a dry river bed," Bridget took it up, feeling she could with them. Then she finished it, "And open a window when you light the gas."

"You've heard."

"I think it's really kind how TEXANS worry about visitors."

"We've lost a lot of them," his mother explained. "And next summer you have to remember to wear a hat in the sun."

"We'll probably be back in Indiana by then." Bridget laughed.

"I'll buy you a hat." J.R. had heard the "probably." She was no longer as positive about leaving. His mother frowned at him. If Bridget was still even *talking* about returning north, either she wasn't interested or he was slow in convincing her.

J.R. drove them back to their house and Lawrence went inside to write to his wife. Jeremy and Bridget walked up the lane with Cassius. She said carefully, "Your family is really nice."

"I agree." Then Jeremy took her hand and asked, "Now what's the matter?"

"You are wealthy."

"There's no harm in having means. We work hard. We're good citizens. You'll have to stay up nights thinking of ways to use our money. It'll give you the freedom to do whatever you want. We can fly to Indiana anytime you want and be there in just a couple of hours. And we'll have a guest house for whenever and whoever you want comes to visit. There isn't any problem we have that we can't solve. I love you, Willis honey." And he "appreciated" her.

The fair could have been called a homecoming. Most of the distant-living kin descended on the area. But it wasn't only kinfolk who showed up. The fair was gathering followers. A family friend, invited the year before, came again and brought another friend, and so it went. Jeremy's three friends from San Antonio came and with their dates; the Taylor cousins came for the first time. The estimated number for that year's attendance was close to three thousand. Now, instead of just covered dishes of food, there was an ox roast. That took a lot of work—three days to prepare and roast—but it was surely worth it.

Inside the barn, tables were set up and handwork shown. Some were just braggings, like Lillian Bates' hand-crocheted tablecloth, but some things were for sale. Bridget bought three deerskin rugs, one for each brother and one for herself, and both she and Lawrence bought a quilt.

They walked around in the crowd and J.R. knew almost everyone. Even the strangers. Little John especially saw to it that he was acquainted. He looked for strangers. It was his business. And everyone was interested in Gus's race.

Bridget teased Jeremy. "You enjoy racing Gus."

"That's just about right. You going to bet on us?" He walked along with his fingers in the back pockets of his jeans.

"We-e-ll, I have to see the other horse."

"You're a faithless woman."

Through the day their particular group of his parents, grandparents, sister and husband, Lawrence and his cousins, the San Antonio friends, Matilda and Mark, Bernice and Little John all met and split to meet with others, and met again. Everywhere they walked, Bridget and J.R. were greeted. J.R. held her hand and the little kids would say, "Hi, J.R.; 'Lo, Miss Taylor, honey."

Jeremy measured Bridget's small hand in his large one as an excuse to hold it and look at her. "Do you know why they say 'hi' to me and ''lo' to you?"

"It has to be a TEXAS joke."

"Pay attention, woman. This is serious and a part of your TEXAS indoctrination. You did realize you would have to go through a series of instruction, didn't you? I'll help. History, legends, that sort of thing. Rules, conduct, manners. You can't just fling yourself into this change. It takes doing."

"Why do they say 'hi' to you and ''lo' to me? I'm braced."

"They say 'hi' to me because I'm bigger. You never grew properly, so they say ''lo' to you since you're closer to the ground. Now if you'd been raised in this rich TEXAS soil . . ."

"It's mostly *rock*."

He could concede that: "We do grow more good TEXAS rock here than in some places in this great state, but look there *between* the rocks."

"Gravel."

"But it's quality gravel."

"Jeremy, you're incorrigible!"

"Sex cures that."
"Nonsense!"
"It's worth the try."

Chapter Nine

It was about ten on the morning of the fair, when the silver trailer with a blue racing stripe arrived. Gus's challenger was brought into the clearing with a flourish, and backed down the trailer's slight ramp. He was a sight! A glistening black stallion who pranced and posed, shook his head, blew and whinnied and rolled his eyes, whistling his own challenge. He was something to see.

Gus was under a tree down a way. He lifted his head halfway up and glanced at the newcomer, then he deliberately, placidly, turned his back end—as if that would be all old blackie would see anyway. But there was a contrast. A few bets were even secretly hedged. Bridget looked at J.R. anxiously, but his face was calm, confident and a little amused.

A man's voice hollered, "Well, J.R., your fifteen minutes are up. By how much?"

Jeremy flicked an indifferent glance at the black beauty and said, "By at least a length and a half."

Then the real betting started among the natives. They knew, most of them, that Gus would win. The bets were on the distance by which he would win. All bets had to be registered with Nina the librarian, who was seated at a table by the door of the building.

When Bridget asked why the bets were registered so carefully, J.R. told her, "About three years ago, it was Gus's first race, and it was a close one. There was some argument about the betting, the cash box disappeared, and everyone got excited. It developed into such a donnybrook, you wouldn't have believed! The broken teeth and heads and knuckles. It was a *scrap*! Even Grandmaw Wilkins got into it. She's no kin— just everyone calls her that. And if it hadn't been for the Reverend Zolar—that man's a spellbinder—he broke out a keg of beer and made everyone sit down so he could talk to us, while Doc Fell patched us up. If old Zolar hadn't been here, it'd probably been the end of Thanksgiving and a lot of friendships. As it is, everyone remembers it rather kindly and with a good deal of droll humor."

"Were you in on that?"

"Oh, yes. But not for long. I was trying to help Little John break it up, and although she's never admitted it, I do believe Grandmaw Wilkins and a chair leg took me out of it early on. I had a goose egg on the back of my head as big as a...goose egg! But..." His eyes narrowed with malicious humor. "I give that ornery old lady a hard time. I pretend I can't remember her name. Like her blow gave me partial amnesia." And he laughed wickedly, very pleased with himself.

"Shame on you."

"I do. And she's always calling me in, saving me a piece of molasses pecan pie, or bringing me the sugared fried doughnut holes that I dearly love, and I say, 'Why thank you, ma'am,' and I very carefully rub where the goose egg was and look perplexed. She blushes like you've never seen!" And he laughed out loud.

"Jeremy," she scolded.

"Serves her right." He tilted back his head and thrust out his lower lip complacently. "A chair leg's just not fair."

It wasn't long before black beauty's owner arrived. He was a stiff, quiet, formal man who couldn't hide his smile at the sight of Gus, down the way.

The race was set for three that sunny afternoon. The time between black beauty's arrival and the race was passed in pleasant anticipation. There were other competitions. Lawrence came in fourth in a horseshoe pitch. Grandmaw Wilkins won a rolling pin throwing contest. J.R. nodded and said, "Figures."

A son of Gus, Uranus, raced in a preliminary event and won. Uranus was beautiful and ran like a poem. One of the young Miner cousins from San Antonio stayed five of the required seven seconds on a meantempered donkey.

The betting on Gus continued, with discussions, arguments, anguishing and even some doubts. Bridget did decide to bet, and she put her money on Gus.

J.R. was smug. "Why'd you decide on Gus?" His voice was silky, wanting to hear her say her reason was himself.

"Loyalty to Gus...who rescued me from the bull."

"*I* rescued you!"

Bridget scoffed. "All you did was lean on the fence and roll cigarettes."

"Willis honey, you *know* you're going to marry me."

"I'm not at all sure."

He offered grudgingly, "If I propose on my knees?" But she only looked at him. He sighed, took her arm and walked her over to the librarian.

"Ahhh, J.R.! Betting on the black horse, right?" she asked saucily, her limpid eyes pools of warm brown humor.

"Now Nina, you know better than that. Have you met my snow bird, Bridget Taylor? Honey, this is Nina.

Nina smiled at her and said, "I've been hearing about you."

"Oh?"

"I have a niece in the first grade: 'That old Mith Tah-lah!'" Nina mimicked a cross child.

Bridget guessed, "Rita?"

"I knew you'd remember Rita. She's had J.R. staked out since she was three."

Nina turned away to register another bet, and J.R. told Bridget, "Rita's is an early case of me. She'll get over me pretty quick. Although, like all the rest, never...quite...entirely."

Bridget clicked her tongue once and slowly shook her head at him.

Nina turned back and picked up her interrupted conversation. "And Doc Fell's nurse is a good friend of mine."

Ah, yes. And with a *late* case of J.R. "She's very pretty." Bridget couldn't think of anything else to say about the nurse.

"She said the same about you." Nina didn't lie, she just didn't quote exactly. "Why'd that damn-Yankee have to be so pretty?" Lissa had raged.

They registered Bridget's bet. Two dollars. J.R. asked after they walked away, "That's all? Now's the time to make your fortune on Gus."

"I was raised to know that betting is not moral."

"Then I salute your crumbling morals and can hardly wait till dark." His teasing voice was husky and his breath was hot on her cheek just before he sneaked a tiny, quick kiss.

She exclaimed and took peeks around to see if anyone was watching...other than the constantly attending first-graders who were giggling, as usual. Then she asked with intense curiosity, but trying to sound off-hand, "When did Nina's case of you happen?"

"Never did." He walked with his hands in his hip pockets.

"One of the two percent?"

"There's always an exception to prove a rule. In fact, I had a brief case of her."

"Early?"

"Not too."

"But you did get over her?"

"Carlo helped. He's her husband now. And big! That man's a giant! And he's mean! They could use him as a boogy man to frighten little kids ... and me. But when he looks at Nina, he gets all wishy-washy. We used to try to tease him about her, but there are healthier ways to pass your time than trying to tease Carlo."

Bridget found she didn't like the idea of Jeremy being interested in another woman, even ten years ago. She frowned over the idea, and he was pleased.

They met with their particular group for lunch. All the handwork that had been for sale had been sold, and the "brags" had been cleared away. Some of the tables had been pulled out from the wall and the staggering amount of food laid invitingly.

Stacks of sliced beef on huge platters were mouth-wateringly ready to eat. They weren't exactly smoked, but had been roasted slowly over coals and gently imbued with the faintly wood-flavored heat and a breath of garlic. Each bite tasted like a need for more. And there was crisp breads, salads and, after a mindless amount of food, still a variety of desserts.

Bridget fretted that Jeremy was eating too much before the race and he should ...

"What," he encouraged lazily.

"Uh, be ... training?"

"How?" He yawned big and long.

"I don't know."

"Neither do I. Relax."

"Well, it isn't *your* two dollars!"

Jeremy threw back his head and laughed out loud, then he had to go around telling everybody that Bridget was alarmed about her two-dollar bet, and even she had to laugh.

Lawrence took pictures of everything to send home to Jean. But Jeremy crawled up in the back of Little John's tacky old pickup to lie down and "rest his eyes."

Bridget helped Grandmaw Wilkins and a score or so of others to put things away and load and unload the dishwasher. Everyone had scraped and stacked their own plates. Grandmaw Wilkins despised paper plates and had donated the dishwasher.

The betting registration was closed as the time for the race approached. J.R. awakened, stomped around, stretched, yawned and rubbed his flat stomach. Bridget found she wanted to rub it for him.

He sleepily smiled at Bridget and wished they were alone. He settled his Stetson on his head, swung his saddle up on his shoulder and clinked down to where Gus stood patiently. Little John and the three San Antonio friends ambled along with him.

The trainer led the black beauty from his improvised stall. That keyed-up and edgy horse pawed, snorted, whistled, tossed his head and danced. He made a lot of people come down with an acute case of the doubts. But Gus turned his head and looked around his shoulder at the black show-off with sagacious tolerance.

In order to mark the track more clearly, they'd borrowed Mrs. Smith's snow fencing from the poles above her parking lot, and to J.R.'s hilarious delight, there was even a video camera to solve a split-decision finish...brought by the challenger. Then a very slender young man saddled the black beauty with a light racing saddle. In contrast, J.R. and his working saddle looked ominously heavy and needlessly bulky on poor old Gus.

Far away, beyond the edge of the clear skies, distant thunder rumbled as if a giant herd of ghost buffalo was running there. Old-timers listened, feeling it in their bodies from the ground, and they narrowed their eyes. "Going to be a gullywasher yonder." But for those at the fair, it only sounded like the opening muffled roll of drums heralding the race.

The Gillis boy's horn sounded in mimicry of The Derby, and was not too badly done, either. Then they all sang *The Eyes of TEXAS*, as J.R. rode Gus around the track. Gus had his nose down, skimming along, inspecting the ground for pot holes. The snorting, sideways-dancing beauty also took a turn and looked magnificent!

The strangers there chuckled, wondering how in the world J.R. had the courage to look so relaxed, in the face of that wondrous challenger, with such a silly looking, scruffy horse. J.R.'s rock-solid granddaddy observed mildly, "Pretty is as pretty does," as his remarkable eyebrows flickered up and down in a knowing way.

Everyone was edging or hurrying for a vantage point as Gus completed his inspection tour of the track and returned to the starting point. There, J.R. stepped down with a creak of leather and that effortlessly smooth flow of muscle. He clinked over to where Bridget stood with their families and friends. His eyes were only for her, and the crinkles around them should have warned her.

He stopped in front of her, removed his Stetson, and held it briefly over his heart as he bowed formally. He opened his arms as he went down on one knee. Bridget's eyes widened. J.R. had caught the eyes of those close around her. He smiled up at her. "My lady, my heart is at your feet."

There was shushings around them, soft questionings and spreading silence as people turned, necks stretched, and interest focused.

"I ask your hand, and may I wear your scarf as the token of your favor?"

In the comparatively small puddle of awareness, very few heard Bridget's waveringly squeaky, "Oh, Jeremy..." as she quickly slid her scarf from her hair. He rose and smiled down at her. With fumbling fingers, she tied her scarf around the upper part of his left arm.

"My son," his dad claimed, and chuckled. "My grandson," claimed the rock, and his mother's voice was tactful. "He's a Winsome all right."

Jeremy and Bridget were only vaguely aware anyone else was on the field. They could have been alone. They and the distance-softened thunder beyond the western horizon.

Jeremy leaned and kissed her soft mouth as he smiled down at her. There were exclamations of approval and laughter among those close by. Then J.R. turned and walked back to Gus, who'd observed the whole episode with as much interest as everyone else.

J.R.'s mother gave Bridget a quick hug around her shoulders and her father clasped her hand as her eyes followed Jeremy. How *could* he do this to her when she was so unsure? But he stepped into the stirrup and swung into the saddle. He again looked at Bridget, and grinned smugly.

Then Gus began his metamorphosis into his legendary image. His head came up with vibrant alertness. His body became alive and fleet. His movements called attention to iron muscles roiling beneath his skin. Silence fell over the watchers. If it hadn't occurred right before their eyes, they would have easily believed another horse had taken Gus's place. He now matched the black beauty with a beauty of his own . . . and he *was* Pegasus.

The gun went off, and Pegasus reared to leap forward an astounding distance which immediately put him in the lead. He floated in a miraculous picture of ease, seeming never to touch the ground, as if in truth Pegasus was flying.

From the starting gun, the race was never in doubt. The black beauty was ignored in his own beautiful run. Not even his owner could tear his eyes from Pegasus, who came in two lengths ahead of his challenger. Again, before their very eyes, he relaxed into the old undistinguished Gus. Bridget's two dollars were safe.

J.R. was subjected to the inevitable pleas to sell Gus, which he turned aside just as inevitably. Gus patiently endured the milling masses who felt the need to touch him—to see if he was real. No one dared go near the nervous prancing black beauty, who was loaded aboard his trailer and carted off.

Those with winning bets couldn't collect their money. They had to wait until the treasurer, Mentor Phebes, puzzled it all out and mailed them checks. A skin-off of ten percent of all winnings over ten dollars was called a "costs fee" and put toward stamps, aspirin—for Mentor took his responsibilities very much to heart—envelopes and the price of next year's ox.

When the crowd around Gus thinned out enough to maneuver, J.R. took Bridget's arm. They led Gus back down under the trees to unsaddle him, walk him, rub him down and pet him.

She asked him, "How much will you win, Jeremy?"

"I never bet," he replied. "I've been raised to know it's morally wrong." Having quoted her exactly, his voice was wrought with humor.

Bridget opened her mouth to retort, but Grandmaw Wilkins came up and brusquely thrust a sack of doughnut "holes" against J.R.'s chest.

"Why, thank you, uh..." J.R. automatically rubbed the back of his head and looked at the lady, sadly puzzled.

"Fraud!" the old lady flung at him with scowling indignation.

"Who told?" he asked in shock.

"That sweet Yankee child."

"Bridget?" he exclaimed, unbelieving. "How *could* you ruin my perfect blackmail like that, honey?"

"I got the recipe."

Jeremy laughed.

"You wretch!" Grandmaw humphed and flounced away.

They ate the holes, coveted them to themselves, but they did share some with Gus.

Excitement was already building for next year's Thanksgiving Fair. J.R. had agreed Gus would race Uranus, who was his son and one heck of a runner too, and everyone thought that would be a race to see.

For supper that evening there were cheese wheels, onion slices, pickles, crisp rolls and butter all laid out with trays of fruit, coffee, beer and soft drinks. Tired and contented, those still reluctant to end the day stood around munching and discussing the next year's race.

The sky above the fairgrounds was beautiful. It would be a lovely cool night full of stars. But far away, in the hidden west beyond the horizon, the thunder rumbled on, like the echo of kettle drums of attacking Turkish horsemen.

Jeremy told Bridget, "The stars are closer to TEXAS than to anywhere else in all the world. Not just little bitty pinpricks, here and there, but you can see them *all*. It's because TEXAS is the first step to heaven." His face was guileless and he frowned reprovingly when she snorted.

Little John and Bernice dropped Bridget off at the Taylor place so she could change into warmer clothes, while J.R. rode Gus home, got his pickup and came to fetch Bridget for star gazing.

When Jeremy tapped on the Taylors' door, he saw Cassius get up from in front of the fire in the living room. He thundered, "Cassius! Just what are you doing in the house?" A smart dog caught sucking eggs couldn't have looked more guilty. "You *know* better!" Jeremy opened the door and held it open and, as Cassius slunk out with his tail between his legs, Jeremy scolded, "Shame on you!"

"Honey?" J.R. turned to Bridget. "Are you trying to ruin a perfectly good dog? He's supposed to be outside, watching things, and you let him lounge around in here?" A look of shock took Jeremy's face. "Have you been letting that hound sleep in your room?"

"Well..."

"On...your bed?"

"Well..." Her squeak higher, she bettered Cassius's guilt.

"You have!" was his positive, horrified accusation.

In a tiny squeak, for the third time she tried, "Well..." Then she added, "Miss Pru..."

"Miss Pru's a lady and pregnant. A hound, Willis honey, is another cup of bouillon! Listen to me, woman, that dog sleeps outside! You hear me? Nothing sleeps in your bed but me! And when we have our passel of little ones, they're going to sleep in their own beds! When I reach for you in the night, I don't want to have to sort through livestock and babies before I get to you!"

He ignored her sputtering, scarlet face, and continued in a perfectly normal voice, "Miss Pru won't count. She'll go back to Mrs. Smith. You might want

to keep one of Miss Pru's kittens...*but it will not sleep
on our bed*. Understand me?''

"I'll think about it.''

"Careful, honey, you're tempting fate.'' She gave
him an aloof look, and he gave her a pat on her nice
round bottom.

Bridget had pulled on black slacks and a white tur-
tleneck sweater. J.R. helped her into a woolen jacket
she'd made from one of the Winsome mill ends she'd
bought from Mrs. Smith. It was a jacket of rich blue
with straight lines and deep pockets. J.R. thought she
was very clever to make it, and he turned her around
in order to admire the jacket, too.

He told her that although she had a tendency toward the corruption of hounds, she was pretty and
talented. He was still sweet-talking her as they drove
out of the yard, leaving a chastened Cassius sitting
forlornly, watching them leave.

Bridget asked J.R. how he'd learned all that sweet
talk, and he replied they were family treasures that
were handed down from father to son. He was surely
glad she'd come along so that he finally had a girl to
practice them on, and his look was so sassy that she
laughed.

She asked him why he loved her, and he said he'd
been helpless before the onslaught of her seduction
when she'd whammied him with the ''Big Eye.''

"My...seduction?''

"Just exactly like Bathsheba's seduction of King
David.''

"She was deliberate.''

J.R. ignored her interruption and speculated musingly, "I wonder if her name was just Sheba before that and someone snidely tacked on the 'bath' after the fateful rinse? Like a mark of Cain or a scarlet letter?"

Bridget disregarded the conversational red herring and was firm in reiteration: "I did not deliberately try to seduce you, Jeremy. If Cassius had been doing his part, I'd have known you were there . . . and . . . those others." Her foggy voice squeaked in remembered embarrassment.

Jeremy grinned and thought to himself that some day he'd have to tell her about those watchers being sheep. But not until she was in the right mood and couldn't escape from him. She'd probably blow sky-high. He chuckled as he continued, "Honey, by the time I saw your gorgeous naked body swinging off that rope above the river, I was already a goner. Your seduction of me started the minute I laid eyes on you and was completed when I listened to you in the store. . . ."

"What? When did you listen to me at the store?"

He ignored her. "So seeing you rise from the river, like Venus on a half shell, was just trimmings. You are a tasty sight, Willis honey. I've been thinking. When we're married I'm going to let you earn our living. You can go on teaching, but full-time, and I'll retire entirely and devote all my time to resting up so's I can make love to you."

"Hah!"

"It's true. I'll have to spend the days resting up for the nights!" His eyes danced wickedly, as he watched her blush and sputter. He continued, his chin up, watching the road, slyly glancing at her now and then. "I figure...how old are you, Willis, honey?"

"Twenty-three October tenth."

He was aghast. "I missed your birthday? Terrible!"

"We weren't here then."

"Well, I can't wait a whole year for another one. I'll think of something. But to go on: Twenty-three? Oh, that's a late start. We'll have our work cut out for us. Hmm. I figure a baby every other year. Okay? That way you'll have our last one when you're about... forty-five or six. How about that?"

"Forty-fi... *twelve*?" Her hoarse voice cracked.

"It'll give you something to do. Teaching and having babies...and making love."

"You're out of your mind!"

"About you. And with twelve it's not too soon to start deciding on names," he cautioned. "I've been giving that considerable thought. How about Truly Winsome. Rather Winsome? Or Very Winsome. Maybe Completely Winsome. Mighty...that would have to be a boy, like Pretty would be a little girl. But there's Fully and Strictly?" His crinkles deepened.

"There's no way I'm going to have twelve kids."

"Eleven?" he bargained, cheerfully undeterred.

She exclaimed a protest.

By then they'd driven to the top of a rise. The night was fantastic, as if God had lavishly strewn handfuls of diamonds through the dark velvet sky. Jeremy made Bridget get back onto the truck bed. She eyed him as he fetched a sleeping bag from the cab and opened it out. He instructed, ''Now. Lie down.''

''Lie down?''

''Of course. How else do you plan to see the stars?'' He was perfectly reasonable. ''There's so many in the TEXAS sky to look at, you'll get a crick in your neck if you're not lying down. Anyway, why else do you think they call it a truck bed?''

''This sounds very much like a new slant on an old dodge.''

He tugged her down as he exclaimed in disgust, ''This is a Ford, not a Dodge! Now you ought to know that. When a male child is born in TEXAS, his daddy swears an oath the child will always drive Ford pickups.''

She scoffed. ''I've seen other makes of pickups.''

''Yankees, every one.''

She laughed.

''It's true. They're trying to infiltrate. I've told you that. They think it's Stetsons and boots and driving pickups that make them one of us, but it's driving Fords. This way we do keep an eye on them. If they ever get smart, squint, roll their own and buy Ford pickups, they'll be just like us. And we wouldn't know they're Yankees . . . except they talk funny.''

''Parents have to swear to a great many obligations down here, don't they.''

''Yep. It's a burden being a parent in TEXAS. That's why, if you're going to be one, you might just as well do a good job of it and have a passel . . . like . . . twelve.''

''Three.''

"That's close enough. Let's get started and then we'll argue how many as we go along." He pulled her flat and kissed her roughly, his hands on her body as she struggled to sit back up.

"Stop that, Jeremy! We're here to see the stars!"

"You're kidding!"

"No. Now behave yourself."

"Man alive! Yankees are strange! Come out to see the stars, and you want to look at the stars? I've never heard of such a thing!" But he obediently pulled her over so that she lay beside him with her head on his shoulder. "You've come to the right man for your astronomy lesson."

"Where's the Little Dipper? I never can find it."

"Over my left shoulder."

"That's the sleeping bag." She was amused by him.

"Not this way." He rolled them over, shifted, pulled her under him and began leisurely to kiss her. It was very comfortable, very nice. She felt that marvelous flicker of pleasure begin inside her body. He lifted his head a fraction and asked against her lips, "Seen it yet?"

"All of them." Her foggy voice was soft and faint.

Chapter Ten

After a while, Jeremy shifted, holding Bridget closer, as his kisses deepened. His voice was husky and roughened. "You do know, Willis honey, that I'm going to seduce you?"

She pushed away from him, and they looked at each other tenderly in the bright starlight. Then she asked, "How would you know how to go about it?" She was so curious how he would reply.

With only an instant's hesitation, he said, "It's an old TEXAS rule: you learn by doing." He took her tenderly into his arms. He kissed her long, deep, lovingly and with great skill. Bridget began to relax, her mouth softened, opening and responding to his kisses. As her arms reached up around his shoulders the Citizens Band radio crackled: "G.K., G.K., you there?" The words were rapped out, quickly.

Jeremy said something under his breath as he released Bridget, heaved up, slid over the side of the pickup and into the cab to punch a button. "Gus's Keeper here, old buddy, what's the problem?"

"Warning! Flash flood from west. Get to high ground soonest."

"Right. We're okay. Tell Bridget Taylor's daddy that she's with me. Need help?"

"All okay. Out."

Jeremy effortlessly swung his body up onto the truck back. "We're sitting in the cat-bird seat. We're going to see a show!"

"What? What are you talking about?"

"All that thunder out west of here today? It wasn't just thunder. It was a gullywasher and all those dry river beds like that one below us there? There'll be a *wall* of water running them. It'll be a sight. You'll see why we all tell strangers to stay out of dry river beds. We'll have ourselves a spectacular."

Just a tad disgruntled, she observed rather cooly, "It must be spectacular if it distracts you from sex."

"Making love," he corrected. Then he said silkily, "I'm not distracted. Now I'll have *time*. With the flood, honey, we're here for the entire night! Remember the stream we forded three or four times? It'll be too deep to cross until sometime tomorrow. I have all night to wear down your resistance." He chuckled and twirled an imaginary mustache.

Bridget's mouth was a soft O, and she questioned in a hoarse little voice, "Jeremy?"

"Yes...Little Nell?"

"Now, Jeremy..."

"Come on, honey, let's watch the show. First things first." Amused teasing rode his voice.

He arranged the sleeping bag in a square and placed it on top of the cab. They sat there with their stockinged feet on the hood of the pickup.

Starlight filled the night with soft silver-brushed magic. It was strangely beautiful, very quiet and nothing seemed to move. They listened. Did they hear a distant roar? The stillness now seemed fraught with tension. Was it really? Or was it because they were aware?

Jeremy's big hand took hers and placed it warm and protected on his thigh. They waited. It was strange. As they watched, clouds began to sneak up from the west, nibbling away at the stars. It seemed there were now furtive rustlings. Were they normal night movements? Or did it only seem ominous to them because they'd been warned of danger? Their senses were heightened. Bridget's nerves stretched, her breath quickened.

There was a roar. Far away but coming closer. She gasped and strained to see. Jeremy pointed. The starlight touched the head of the encroaching wave of disaster with silver, highlighting it. Spotlighting it. "Oh, Jeremy." She breathed in awe and watched fascinated as the "snake" of silver writhed closer, and the sound became louder. Closer—closer—mounting—frightening. Panic! Almost without thought, she instinctively wanted to flee the sound, which mounted into a thundering roar.

Friction with the dry bed held the bottom of the water wall so that the hurrying top collapsed downward, to in turn be overrun. The silver tide burst around the peak where they were, dividing with a slapping, grinding, moblike roar. The flood fled on, leaving an agitated, whispering, slurpy, gurgling rush that followed swiftly. It was a stunning experience.

They watched for a long time, then the waters seemed to deepen with an additional surge. Very soon after that, there was a perceptible slowing of its headlong rush under clouds that were now rapidly blotting out the stars.

Jeremy stood up on the hood of the truck and watched intently. "We may be here longer than just overnight."

"Why? What do you mean?" Her questions were faint and fogged.

"I'd guess that earthen dam about ten miles west of here finally gave out.... That second wave of water? And now it's slowed down so much that there must be a slide east of here that's holding some back. That'll help the folks on down the river, but it might hamper us just a trifle."

The high clouds were slowly pulled across the sky like a black blanket whose forward edge was grayed blue. As the stars vanished behind it the darkness increased, until very soon it was pitch black. They couldn't even see each other.

Jeremy raised Bridget to her feet and kissed her. "There's nothing for you to worry about, honey. I've always carried a change of clothes, blankets, a rope, survival food and water. We could last a glorious week out here. But the choppers will be out tomorrow scouring the area for victims. They'll most likely be here by dawn's early light, so let's not be wasting good time, Willis honey, let's get to bed."

"But Jeremy...I'm...afraid."

"Aw, honey, there's no need. You know I love you. I wouldn't hurt you for all the world. Everyone knows I'm going to marry you. You do love me, don't you? Willis," he questioned sharply, "you're not trying to tell me you don't!"

"I do, but..."

"Then there's no problem. I promise we won't start on the twelve...yet." J.R. arranged the sleeping bag by feel. Bridget strained her eyes into the total darkness, trying to see anything at all. She heaved a big sigh. "I guess walking home is out."

Jeremy laughed. "Now, honey, don't sound so pitiful. By morning you'll be hanging on me begging for more, and I'll be all played out and pleading to be let alone to sleep. Anyway, you daren't step down from the truck in the dark. With the rising waters, the snakes will be thick as fleas out there."

"Snakes...."

"Yep. Even in this paradise there are snakes."

"But..." She showed a definite lack of conversational variance and her hoarse voice trailed off.

He busily climbed over and swung into the cab without touching the ground. He rooted around in the space behind the cab seat and came back the same way. "Orange juice," he explained. "Sit down here and drink it," he coaxed. "You'll feel better. All in all, it's been quite a day of shocks: betting a whole two

dollars on Gus and me; being proposed to in public—
and on my knees."

"Only one knee."

"It still counts. Seeing a gullywasher. And, heh heh
heh, being marooned on an island with a raging sex
fiend!"

She didn't know whether to laugh or cry. "Jeremy,
this is very embarrassing, but I…have to…comb my
eyebrows."

There was a brief silence before he asked, "Huh?"
Then almost immediately he said, "Oh, the old sand-
box. Mmm." He considered the problem. Very reluctantly he agreed, "I'll turn on the headlights, you'll
wear my boots, and don't you *dare* to leave the lights'
path. You hear? Be sure you stomp around good be-
forehand. Honey, it's cold and it's night, but those
snakes are all upset. Be careful!"

"I will." By then she was thoroughly frightened.

"At least let me go stomp around first." He did,
endlessly. Then he put his boots on her for her trip into
the headlights.

It seemed to him she took forever. When she returned to the side of the truck, he reached down and
lifted her bodily, swiftly, onto the truck. "Are you all
right?" His hands on her shoulders, he shook her a
little.

She was startled to feel how he trembled as he held
her tightly against him.

"My God, you'll be the death of me. You may drink
only a *sip* of that orange juice! I'm not going through
that again tonight."

He kissed her rather roughly three or four times, his breathing still disturbed and his hands still unsteady from his fear for her. He took his boots off her and set them against the cab. In the reflected glow of the headlights, she watched him skim over into the cab to turn off the lights.

As he was returning, he suddenly stopped dead still and said intensely, "Listen!"

They even held their breaths. Bridget was in terror, not knowing why they were listening.

It came. A different splash!

J.R. reached into the cab and pulled the headlights back on. He flung himself into the truck bed and jerked on his boots. He tore into the cab, ripped out an emergency flashlight, the coil of rope, and he put on his holster and gun.

His voice boomed in the stillness. "Where are you, boy?"

Absolutely still, they listened tensely.

"Stay here!" He rapped the command to Bridget and leaped down from the truck. In the dark, the bobbing light went swiftly down through the scrub toward the water. Bridget's hands went out toward his retreating figure to stop him. Who was out there? What had he heard to give him direction?

It was Jeremy out there, crashing through the underbrush with the snakes and God-only-knew what all. There was someone in the water. Now it was she who worried and shivered. She dared not call—or follow. Would Jeremy be so foolish as to go into the water? Where was he?

An endless time later, she saw the bobbing light far off to the left, picking an uncertain way back to the truck. "Jeremy?" she squeaked, as they came closer. *They.* She could see two shapes in the glow cast by the unsteady light.

J.R.'s breathless voice puffed. "It's Little John... he's okay...just a bit tired. What a night...for a swim...you dunderhead. Come on...just a little more. 'Atta boy...we're almost there." Jeremy's breath was labored. "Honey...grab his arms...and pull...when I lean him. I'll push. Lord...man...you weigh a ton!"

They huffed and puffed and got him onto the truck bed, a deadweight. Little John, shivering with exhaustion and shock, was no help at all.

"There's towels behind the seat. Get a couple?" and he began to strip off Little John's wet clothes. Bridget returned quickly. "Rub his back and hair *hard.*" Jeremy was vigorously hand rubbing Little John's legs and arms, coaxing circulation. Then he took the towel and quickly dried Little John so they could slip him into the sleeping bag.

Jeremy talked to Little John in a calming, chaffing way the entire time, finally making Little John raise himself on an elbow and drink the can of orange juice. Then they put blankets over the sleeping bag.

Little John muttered, "Your headlights...I thought I was...a goner." His words blurred, and he was asleep.

J.R. turned off the headlights but left the dome light on as a beacon to anyone else. He punched the CB radio, listened to the chatter, then said, "Breaker, Breaker, G.K. calling Jammer?"

"Yeah, J.R.?"

"Tell Bridget Taylor's daddy she's safe as she'd be in church? Little John just swam in."

"My Lord! We've been worried sick! He okay?"

"Tired, but we've got him dry and snug, and he's asleep. Tell his folks . . . and Bernice?"

Bridget realized J.R. was soaked, too. They rooted around and found a jacket and some scruffy but dry trousers and socks. J.R. stripped and put on the dry things and lay his and Little John's wet clothes out on the hood and on the top of the cab. Then he and Bridget climbed into the cab, started the motor and ran the heater until the cab was cozy, then turned it off. Bridget said Little John should be in the cab. J.R. replied he'd done well to just get him up that hill, but he couldn't wrestle him into the cab if his life depended on it.

They periodically checked Little John to be sure he was warm and breathing okay—he'd swallowed a lot of water. Finally they could remove the extra blankets and let him sleep in just the sleeping bag.

They sat in the cab intertwined, kissing. She told him, "I was afraid for you."

"That's because you love me. And you'll love being a TEXAN. You will marry me?"

"Oh, Jeremy, I love you so."

"Enough?"

"Yes."

"Well, thank God you're smart enough to realize that!"

They talked about their future. "Will you want to paint the home place?"

"I think I like the way the boards look now; could we just put preservative on it?"

"It'd soak up a gallon per square inch!"

And now and then they even dozed.

In the early morning, Little John wakened and seemed not much worse for his experience. He complained because J.R. hadn't found his boots. His shirt was dry enough and he pulled on his still-damp trousers.

J.R. built a fire and, during the morning, killed off seven snakes—one a beautiful jewel of a king coral. The snakes gave Bridget the shudders, especially since he draped them over a bush. So she mostly stayed on the truck bed.

Little John explained why he'd been out. He'd been sure the Garcia family had gotten out—but not quite sure enough. They had no phone so, shaving it close, he'd gone to check on them. When he saw their chicken coop was on their roof, he knew they'd been warned and were all right.

Coming back he'd blown a tire and swerved, smacked into a boulder and gotten well and thoroughly stuck. He'd hot-footed it for high ground, and almost made Lonesome Oak hill when the wall of water hit. He'd managed to leap up. "I hadn't realized I could jump that high," he said. Grabbing a scrubby bush he'd survived the initial onslaught, but the dry ground around the bush's roots gradually crumbled away. He'd struggled to shed his holster and boots before the bush gave up.

He was swept along as the stars disappeared and in the total dark, especially with the almost complete loss of current, he couldn't tell which way to swim. He was about done in, when he saw their headlights. He'd felt pure terror when they'd gone out...

While Little John talked, J.R. made beef soup from a survivor packet of dried vegetables and beef boullion. Then he brewed coffee and tea for Bridget. Jeremy bellyached the entire time: "Hell, here I got Bridget in a compromising situation, and you have to swim in! Why don't you wade out into the flood waters until your hat floats away?"

Little John chided, "That's an unfriendly thing for you to say, J.R., and anyway, God only knows where my hat's floating right now."

J.R. groused, "I don't feel friendly, and on top of everything else, now I have to feed you!"

Little John tasted the soup and suggested it had too much salt. Then he argued, "Since I'm the marshal here, I should get to wear our boots. If I go on walking around in my stocking feet, I just might step on a stickerburr."

Jeremy huffed, "Now just a cotton-picking minute, those aren't our boots, they are solely, get that play on words, mine!"

From the truck bed, Bridget listened and knew they must always speak in that bantering way.

The two men took long sticks and cautiously poked around in the truck's engine and underneath it to be sure it harbored no creepy visitors. Via the CB they declined the helicopter, saying there were fine. "Too

cozy," was J.R.'s comment. He said they could be
rescued.

J.R. and Little John kept the snakes' rattlers for
Bridget's brothers and, on sticks, roasted some of the
meat for lunch. They tried to coax Bridget into trying
some. "It tastes just like chicken." But that only made
her suspicious of everything else they cooked.

They tidied up at suppertime, left the dome light on
in the cab, the key in the ignition and the doors un-
locked in case anyone needed shelter, food, heat or the
CB. It was getting on toward dark when the chopper
came for them. There was no place to land so they
were told they would have to climb the ladder. Bridget held back.

The young technician skimmed down to hold the
ladder steady. J.R. and Little John were familiar with
helicopters. They were urged to be quick about it, the
chopper was low on fuel. Little John scurried up the
ladder. Bridget watched. J.R. told her to go on now,
but she held back. Shouts from above warned them to
hurry. She said for Jeremy to go on, that she'd go
next. She watched the uncertain balance of the ladder
as J.R. went on up. She refused to follow.

The technician commanded her to climb, and J.R.
yelled, but Bridget backed away in the prop wash. J.R.
almost went back down, but the technician was going
up so Little John prudently held J.R. back. Time ran
out. The technician scrambled up the rest of the way
as the pilot took off.

The chopper dipped and swerved and Bridget
watched in horror, thinking it would crash, but it

steadied and flew away into the rapidly darkening, overcast night.

And she was alone.

Chapter Eleven

The helicopter's whomp, whomp, whomp soon became a distant flutter and the silence closed down. All the little creatures were still—frozen by the chopper's loud intrusion.

Bridget looked around and became increasingly aware of her situation. She was completely alone and night was coming on. Alarmed, she climbed quickly into the cab, slammed and locked both doors. She sat stock-still and big-eyed, jerking her head around at any whisper of sound.

With the overcast skies, the night was again pitch black. Bridget became a bit teary-eyed because she was afraid and all by herself. She sniffed, her heart thundered, and she decided she was probably hungry.

She refused to even consider getting out of the truck again until daylight. She poked around, rejecting

anything that would have to be cooked, and found a
dried bread rusk. She nibbled on that, and tried to
swallow it as she gave herself a mental scolding. So she
was a city girl, but she was a Taylor! She thought of
the pioneer women. They hadn't been able to see any
lights when they looked outside at night, and they'd
had Indians to worry about.

Thinking about hostiles was a mistake. Up until
then, she'd really only worried about snakes and a selected choice of animals, all four-legged, like lions,
tigers and bears. There weren't any bears or tigers
running around loose in TEXAS. Her imagination
then peopled the underbrush with attackers and mur-
derers or a combination thereof. She was rapidly becoming a basket case.

She reasoned with herself that although Jeremy
found her tempting, no one else would struggle
through that flood-torn, waterlogged countryside just
for a taste of her. She turned off the dome light. No
sense in advertising.

Finally she took one of the blankets, and wrapped
in it, she lay across the seat to rest. A soft cold rain
began to fall, the sound on the cab roof enclosed her
cocoonlike. Finally exhausted, she slept.

"Jammer calling Bridget Taylor?"

She roused herself from sleep and for several seconds felt like an amnesia victim, until she sorted out
where she was and why.

"Punch the red button and tell me you're there.
Release it to hear me."

"Uh. Hello?"

A different voice replied, "Bridget, sugar? This is Doctor Fell. Are you all right?"

"Yes." She remembered to press the button. "Yes."

"Sugar, J.R. and Gus are missing and—"

"What!" The button. "What?"

The old man's calm voice said, "We think J.R.'s trying to get back to you? If he shows up, will you call me? Anytime, now, as I'll be sleeping here."

"All right."

Gently, he asked again, "You are all right? Can you stay there until morning? The chopper has something loose, and they can't get you until then."

"I'm fine." Her voice a tiny, husky sound.

"Good girl. Now you be sure to call in if he shows up there, won't you? We'll be looking for him around here."

"Okay."

"'Night now. Try to sleep. If we find him, we'll call you and let you know where he is."

"All right...and thank you."

Sleep? She was wide awake, worried and scared. How had all this happened anyway and *where was Jeremy*? As she thought about him, she faced the fact she'd subconsciously known all along: nothing else in her life was as important as he was to her. He was no brief affair, to sample and go blithely on her way. She truly loved him, as much as she'd resisted acknowledging it. But had she realized that too late?

Two dark, praying, silent hours later, a sound came faintly to her ears. She hesitantly opened the cab window a crack and listened, holding her breath. Nothing.

The rain had stopped, the clouds were breaking up
and here and there was a star. She opened the door and
stood on the step to look around, listening, and feeling like the last human being on earth.

There! She was sure she'd heard something! Again
she strained her ears ... and she heard her heart beating. Otherwise there was only silence.

It was! A shrill whistle sounded, smothered by distance and, "... lis!" faintly, far away, like a ghost
whisper.

At the top of her rusty, foggy, cracking vocal
chords, she screamed, *"Jeremy! Jer-e-meee!"* setting
off a skittering in the bushes she didn't even hear, she
was so concentrated on distant sound....

And there was an answering whistle.

She pulled on the lights and unsnapped the truck
bed cover to climb up there, then she swung the emergency light wailing, "Jeremy!" from the top of her
lungs and the bottom of her heart.

Cassius got there first. He shook water from his
coat and barked once. It was the first bark she'd ever
heard from him. Then, carefully judging the height,
he jumped onto the truck bed. Bridget burst into tears
and hugged the wet dog who held still for her em-
brace. He was exhausted and flopped down panting.

Twisting and straining, Bridget stood on tiptoe to
gain another inch or so. "Jeremy!"

"He-e-e-y-y, Will-lli-i-s-s!" He was getting closer.

She held the light straight up and finally heard the
faint splash of a large creature, and Jeremy's voice
encouraging Gus. There was a churning, a splashing,
then the heave of the body from water and finally the

clop of cautious hooves as Gus picked his careful way to the truck.

Bridget's voice was quavering. "Oh, Jeremy... Oh...oh, Jeremy." She was not even aware she spoke.

The tired horse and man finally came into shadowy view, and Bridget had to resist flooding them in the emergency light and blinding them.

"Hi, honey. You okay?" He was anxious and worn.

"Fine. Oh, Jeremy."

"Stay up there!" he cautioned sharply. "Let me get this saddle off this good ole horse." He slowly dismounted, uncinched the saddle, dragged it off and heaved it astraddle the side of the truck. Then he took Gus's bridle off and patted his neck. "Man, I sure do owe these two." He climbed the cab step wearily and stepped over into the truck bed.

Bridget flung herself at him so that he staggered against the back of the cab as his arms closed around her, and he half sat on it as she clung to him. Realization came to her. "You're soaked! Take off those clothes this minute!"

His voice dragged. "I'm glad to see you're finally eager to get me out of my clothes, Willis honey, but I'm so worn out, I'm not sure I could rise to the occasion."

She wasn't listening to him but busily got a blanket from the cab and began to help him pull off his wet boots.

"I brought you something." He slowly unbuttoned his shirt pocket.

She was trying to get his wet socks off. He was languid and patient. She put his boots upside down and

draped his socks over the truck side. Cassius watche
her with the same lassitude. Gus stood still by th
truck, his head really drooping.

"Your birthday present...one of the Australia
opals." He took her left hand, slipped the ring on he
finger and said, "That will serve double duty until
get my great-grandmother's ring from the bank." H
kissed her carefully.

She rather distractedly kissed him back as she u
buttoned his shirt. "Here, you do this, I've got to te
them you're here. And I'll start the motor and get th
heater going, you've got to get warm."

"I'm all right. Just a trifle tired. You are such a tri
to me, woman. Why didn't you get on that cho
per?"

"I was afraid." A Taylor admitting to being afraid
She helped him out of his shirt and spread it on top
the cab.

Lethargically he told her, "Bernice is cured of m
entirely."

"Is she?" She wasn't paying close attention.

"Yep. We landed and she was there, and she didn
even see me. She just 'flanged' herself at Little Joh
He was so smug." J.R. chuckled lazily.

"I was so worried about you."

"About me?" That surprised him.

"Dr. Fell called and said you'd disappeared."

"Oh, that." He dismissed that. "You glad to s
me?" His voice was husky, he hugged her briefl
"You worried about me?"

"Just feel my heart beat." Then she scolded, "N
there, here in my throat."

"You do it your way; I'll do it mine."

"It couldn't *possibly* be there!"

"Well, it's bound to turn up somewhere." He continued his leisurely search.

"You know it's here!"

"To blindly accept someone else's word is to have a closed mind." He yawned and winced. "Doubt and personal investigation are vital to the freedom of this great country of ours."

"I love you, Jeremy." She gave him an earnest, hard kiss.

"Ouch!"

"What's the matter?"

"It's just my jaw. Little John had to knock me out."

"What! That beast! After you saved his life! How dare he!"

He laughed, carefully. "Honey, simmer down. I was trying to wreck the chopper to get back to you, and I must have gone a little around the bend, insisting like I did that I wanted out of that crate. They couldn't get back to you, didn't have enough gas. I was getting to be a nasty problem, so Little John solved it." He yawned hugely and groaned because his jaw didn't like doing that. "I've got to stretch out. I'm done wore out."

She hurried to spread the sleeping bag on the truck bed, and he slid out of his trousers as he got into it. He slept almost immediately. Both animals rested.

In the silence, Bridget watched Jeremy, then spread his trousers on the cab roof and went to turn off the truck lights. Then she remembered Dr. Fell's admonition to call him. She punched the button on the CB and said, "This is Bridget Taylor. May I speak to Dr. Fell?"

"Hold on just a minute. Everything all right there?"

"Yes. Jeremy's here."

"Well, thank God for that. Here's the doc."

"Sugar?" began the sleepy old man.

"He's here. He's asleep."

"Is he all right?"

"Very tired."

"He has a concussion."

"What!"

"He'd been given a shot, and he was supposed to stay in bed at the clinic, where I could keep an eye on him, but he escaped. That shot should have knocked him out entirely. We'd had to wrestle him some in order to give it to him, and when he took off, we worried if the shot might catch up to him some place inconvenient. I didn't mention it sooner. I didn't want to worry you."

"He got here first."

"Well, we surely do thank God for that. He'll probably have a terrible headache tomorrow. Do you have any aspirin?"

"There's some in the first-aid kit."

"Do you have enough?"

"Let me see. Yes, I think so."

"Good. He'll most likely sleep heavily until late afternoon. You might turn him over in a couple of hours or he'll be stiff."

"All right. How'd he get the concussion?"

He replied placidly, "When he was trying to hijack the helicopter, and Little John stopped him, he hit his head. If he hadn't done that, he'd have probably jumped out into the floodwaters to swim back to you. You know how chancy that would have been, with all the debris in the water? The boy was some upset, leaving you there alone." There was a sleepy chuckle. "We won't fetch you back until tomorrow...er... this evening. I'd rather he sleep undisturbed. We'll come out if you need us—if he can't be roused—but I'm glad you don't need us. We could get there, but it would be tricky on foot. The helicopter is being fixed and it would take a while. You are all right?"

"Don't worry about us." They said good-night, Bridget turned off the lights and climbed back onto the truck bed. She was dead tired. She decided if Jeremy was that drugged, and he'd sleep twelve hours, she might just as well get some sleep, too. She eased into the sleeping bag; he didn't move, and she curled against his back in the cool dark night. She had a vagrant thought: here they were in the same sleeping bag, and he was sleeping off a potent shot. "I do not like thee, Dr. Fell..." Drowsy, she heard Cassius leave the truck. Secure and cozy against Jeremy's warm back, she drifted off into sleep.

With the dawn, she opened her eyes to look up into Jeremy's watching face and smiled back at him. She thought, twelve hours, indeed. She gently touched his left eye which was swollen shut and bruised. His jaw was lopsided and dark, too, with a great bruise. "Your poor face."

"I could tell it was going to be a sight, so I came back so's I'd be compromised. I'll look so beaten up, and there you'll be without a . . . visible mark. I'll tell everyone I sure did put up a good fight but that you ravished me, and—"

"*I*"

"And you'll have to marry me. No one else would have me so obviously secondhand and shopworn, like I'll look." He leaned to kiss her as he grinned lopsidedly. His hand slowly appreciated her. He settled her back down, with him leaning over her, and her arms curled around him, welcoming him.

He inquired as to whether she'd adjusted to the promise of his seduction? And he watched the dawn mark her blush.

"But you shouldn't have come back." Her fingers moved in his hair in a caressing way.

"No?"

"I am glad you're here. But with that shot, you could have been killed, falling off Gus or not ducking a branch. You took a terrible chance."

"I just couldn't abide that mattress at the clinic. I told you about them. I knew you'd be lots softer. Ummmmm. See? Nice. Do you happen to suspect that my interest might lean in your direction?"

"There's been a hint or two."

"Umm. You are nice."

"I'd have died if anything had happened to you."

"I had Gus and Cassius, so I was safe. It was you out here, all alone, that caused me the shivering horrors. I just had to get to you. I love you more than my life, Willis honey. Even more than Gus. But let's not risk him again...you could upset our whole economy."

"Oh, honey." She wasn't aware she'd used the word, but J.R. smiled, absolutely charmed by her calling him that.

Lazily he gloated, "So you've *finally* joined the ninety-eight percent."

She agreed, "You're irresistible." Her foggy voice was soft. Her lips parted, their tongues touched, and the heat rose from the sleeping bag, turning to steam in the cold air. It was the beginning of their long, good years together.

* * * * *

Silhouette Romance

Next month some of your all-time favorites are returning to the Silhouette Romance Line. And the celebration doesn't end there— next we have the month of continuing stars. Don't miss it—come home to Romance.

"Homecoming Celebration"

COMING NEXT MONTH

#526 RUN TO ME—Parris Afton Bonds
Jaclyn Richardson had come to the reservation to hide. But could she hide her love for handsome detective Joe Watchman, her savior—the one man she could never have?

#527 A MATTER OF TIMING—Dixie Browning
Janey Abbott loved a good cause, so how could she resist Avery? But was Avery more than he seemed—and could Janey find love in the right place at the wrong time?

#528 TOO CLOSE FOR COMFORT—Brooke Hastings
Jessica Lawrence had to be lured out of town for her own protection and without her knowledge. Detective Griff Marshall was the man for the job, until he fell out of character—and in love.

#529 TEMPTATION—Nora Roberts
Running a girls' camp drove Eden Carlbough up a tree—and crashing into the arms of handsome Chase Elliot. One look at Eden, and Chase knew he didn't want to be the serpent in her paradise....

#530 STOLEN TRUST—Sondra Stanford
Alan Daniels had left Rose Bennington long ago, but now fate gave them a second chance. Rose still loved Alan, but she couldn't trust him—or could she?

#531 BROKEN DREAMS—Jeanne Stephens
Wyatt and Kristin Knowles's marriage had fallen apart because of Wyatt's dangerous career. But now Wyatt was back and determined to build a new dream: a life with Kristin.

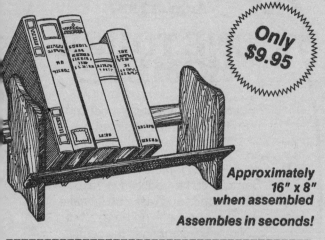